THE ROYAL BALLET SCHOOL

Diaries 7

Second Year

New Girl

D1470326

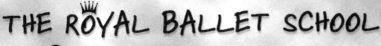

THE ROYAL BALLET SCHOOL
Diaries
7
Second Year

New Girl

Written by Alexandra Moss

Grosset & Dunlap

Special thanks to Sue Mongredien

For the real Alice Granlund, with lots of love

GROSSET & DUNLAP
Published by the Penguin Group
Penguin Group (USA) Inc., 375 Hudson Street, New York, New York 10014, U.S.A.
Penguin Group (Canada), 90 Eglinton Avenue East, Suite 700, Toronto, Ontario, Canada M4P 2Y3
(a division of Pearson Penguin Canada Inc.)
Penguin Books Ltd, 80 Strand, London WC2R 0RL, England
Penguin Ireland, 25 St Stephen's Green, Dublin 2, Ireland
(a division of Penguin Books Ltd)
Penguin Group (Australia), 250 Camberwell Road, Camberwell, Victoria 3124, Australia
(a division of Pearson Australia Group Pty Ltd)
Penguin Books India Pvt Ltd, 11 Community Centre, Panchsheel Park, New Delhi - 110 017, India
Penguin Group (NZ), Cnr Airborne and Rosedale Roads, Albany, Auckland 1310, New Zealand
(a division of Pearson New Zealand Ltd)
Penguin Books (South Africa) (Pty) Ltd, 24 Sturdee Avenue, Rosebank, Johannesburg 2196, South Africa

Penguin Books Ltd, Registered Offices:
80 Strand, London WC2R 0RL, England

Series created by Working Partners Ltd.

Copyright © 2006 by Working Partners Ltd. All rights reserved. Published by Grosset & Dunlap, a division of Penguin Young Readers Group, 345 Hudson Street, New York, New York 10014. GROSSET & DUNLAP is a trademark of Penguin Group (USA) Inc. Printed in the U.S.A.

Moss, Alexandra.
New girl / written by Alexandra Moss.
p. cm. — (The Royal Ballet School diaries ; 7)
Summary: Now in Year 8 at The Royal Ballet School, Ellie tries to make the new girl in her class feel welcome while also learning how to deal with her feelings for her classmate, Luke.
ISBN 0-448-44250-7 (pbk.)
[1. Ballet dancing—Fiction. 2. Interpersonal relations—Fiction. 3. Boarding schools—Fiction. 4. Schools—Fiction. 5. Royal Ballet. School—Fiction.] I. Title. II. Series.
PZ7.M8515New 2006
[Fic]—dc22
2005035924

10 9 8 7 6 5 4 3 2 1

Chapter

1

Dear Diary,

I am sooo excited! This is the last day of the summer vacation, and tomorrow I'm going back to The Royal Ballet School—as a Year 8 student! I won't be one of the youngest there any longer. A whole class of new students will be arriving there today, all nervous and excited—just like I was, last September.

I just can't wait to see all my school friends again: Grace, Lara, Isabelle, Bryony, Kate, and the others. And as well as catching up on all their news, I am desperate to get back to regular ballet classes, too. I've been practicing as hard as I can at the barre I've got in my bedroom here in Oxford, but it's not the same as being in a studio, with a teacher and a pianist and the other students all inspiring me to dance my very best! Roll on our first class . . . it just can't come soon enough!

I feel a bit sad, though, that we won't be having ballet class with Ms. Wells anymore. She'll be teaching the new Year 7s. I learned so much from her and feel like she knows all of us girls inside out now. Our new ballet teacher is Ms. Black. Jessica, my guide, was taught by her last year and told me that she really enjoyed having class with her. I hope I like her, too—and that she likes me!

Also, I'm dying to see which dormitory I've been allocated, and whom I'm going to be sharing with. Last year I shared the huge Year 7 dorm with all the other Year 7 girls, but this year we get split into two smaller dorms. Most of us will be in the Billiard Room—which really WAS once a billiard room! That was years and years ago, though—back in the days when White Lodge was a king's royal hunting lodge. The Billiard Room is divided into two areas—the West End and the East End—and there's also a long, narrow dorm leading off from there, known as the "Room Off." I can't

decide which would be more fun: to be part
of the bigger Billiard Room dorm, or to be
in the cozy little Room Off, with just three
other people. Well, one thing's for sure: I'll
find out tomorrow.

I so hope I've been put with Grace,
whichever dorm I get. At the end of last
term, we each got to nominate (secretly!)
four girls we'd most like to share with. I put
down Grace, Lara, Bryony, and Isabelle.
Mrs. Hall, our housemother from last year,
promised us we'd get put with at least one
person from our list, and hopefully more.

It felt strange not being able to put
Sophie on my list. I feel really sad that she
won't be coming back to school with us this
year. She is definitely one of my favorite
people. It still makes me sad that she was
"assessed out" last year. Year 8 is certainly
going to be quieter without her. I'll really
miss her laugh, her singing, her hilarious
impressions—and, of course, her horoscope
predictions, even if they were never exactly
accurate! Still, I know that she's really
psyched about starting at her new
performing arts school up in Manchester.

She's going to love it, I'm sure—and the other students will all totally love her. I'm already looking forward to getting one of her funny cards or e-mails, telling me how it's all going. Sophie Crawford is going to be my friend forever—and that's a definite.

I'd better finish packing, I guess! I keep looking over at my open suitcase and seeing my new Year 8 ballet uniform packed in there. I just love the cornflower blue leotard and ballet skirt—and we have pink tights instead of socks now—much more grown-up! I can't wait to wear it all in class.

Oh, won't it be strange at first, though, seeing all the new Year 7 girls wearing pink instead of me and my classmates??

Signing off—until I sign on again tomorrow—as a Royal Ballet School Year 8 student!

•   •   •   •

It was very strange the next day, arriving back at The Royal Ballet School's Lower School and not heading straight across the airy reception hall to the Year 7 dorm entrance, just off to the right. Instead, Ellie led her mom up the curving marble staircase toward the three Year 8 dorms. She allowed herself just one backward glance in the direction of the Year 7 dorm—and caught a glimpse of two very wide-eyed girls emerging from it together.

"Look," she murmured to her mom. "They must be two of the new Year 7s—boy, do they look nervous." Ellie felt a pang of sympathy for them. She'd never forget how overwhelmed she'd felt arriving at The Royal Ballet School as a new student. Exciting—yes, and exhilarating, too—but at the same time it was totally exhausting trying to take everything in and remember everybody's name.

She flashed a smile at the new girls, wanting to be as welcoming as possible. It hardly seemed any time at all since she had been in their position.

"It takes me right back," her mom commented. "I can remember so clearly dropping you off here and driving away. I had to pull over about three times, I was sobbing so much. I hated leaving my baby behind."

"Awww, Mom . . ." Ellie said, grinning at her. "You won't be sobbing again today, will you?"

Her mom laughed. "Of course not," she said. "Not now that I know just how much you love being here."

They turned into a corridor, and there at the end of it, on the left, was the Year 8 girls' Slip—the room that led on to the dormitories.

Ellie pushed open the Slip door and she and her mom went inside. It looked very much like the Year 7 Slip, with a desk for the housemother—their *new* housemother, Mrs. Parrish, Ellie reminded herself—some lockers, a sofa, a piano, and a notice board.

Heart thumping, Ellie made a beeline for the notice board to find the dorms list she had been told would be waiting there. It was pinned in the center of the board.

Billiard Room:

Bed 1: Scarlett Briggs

Bed 2: Rebecca Todd

Bed 3: Alice Granlund

Bed 4: Holly Powell

Bed 5: Megan Paltrow

Bed 6: Lara McCloud

Bed 7: Kate Walker

Bed 8: Isabelle Armand

Ellie smiled. Lara, Kate, and Isabelle were all together. She knew they'd be pleased about that. She continued looking down the list.

Room Off:

Bed 1: Bryony Andrews

Bed 2: Grace Tennant

Bed 3: Ellie Brown . . .

Aha! There she was. Yaay! She was sharing with Grace and Bryony—in a room to themselves! And then her eyebrows shot up in surprise as she realized there was a name below hers. A name she didn't know.

Bed 4: Molly Baker

"Molly Baker?" she read aloud.

"Who's Molly Baker?" her mom asked curiously, looking at the list, too.

"I've got no idea," Ellie replied. Molly Baker. It was there in black and white. "But I'm sleeping next to her, whoever she is!" she added.

Ellie and her mom pushed through the door that led into the Billiard Room. There, unpacking with her mom at Bed 4, was a new girl. Molly Baker!

Ellie realized what had happened. The school must have filled Sophie's place. Her mind whirling, she walked over. "Molly?" she asked tentatively. "I'm Ellie. Um . . . welcome to The Royal Ballet School!"

Molly looked up and smiled at once, a huge grin stretching below her sparkly brown eyes. "Hi!" she said, abandoning her unpacking and rushing over to Ellie. "Ellie, did you say? Oh, I'm so relieved someone else has arrived!" Molly grinned hello to Mrs. Brown, and then turned back to Ellie. "Mum and I got here about an hour ago—isn't it gorgeous, this place? And Mrs. Parrish showed us here—she's lovely, isn't she? And neither of us has dared go off exploring because we thought we'd get lost straightaway, so I've been hoping and hoping one of my dorm-mates would get here soon—and here you are!"

"Yes, here I am!" Ellie laughed, lifting her case onto her new bed next to Molly's. Molly sure could talk! But if first impressions were anything to go by, Ellie was going to like her chatty new dorm-mate.

"Can I leave you in Ellie's safe hands, then, Moll?" Molly's mom asked, coming over to hug her daughter. "If I can find my way out of here again, that is!" she chuckled.

"I'll show you the way out," Ellie's mom offered at once. "It takes a bit of getting used to, this school—it's something of a rabbit warren, isn't it?"

Molly's mom smiled. "You can say that again. I said to Molly we should have dropped pieces of bread behind us in a trail, like Hansel and Gretel, when Mrs. Parrish led us to the dorm!"

Ellie's mom laughed, and then turned to Ellie. "Bye then, sweetie," she said, hugging her hard. "I know you'll have fun. Call me tomorrow, won't you, to tell me how your first day as a Year 8 went?"

"Sure," Ellie said, wrapping her arms tightly around her mom. "Bye!"

The two moms went out of the dorm, and Ellie turned to Molly expectantly. "So . . ." she began, but just at that moment,

Grace walked in. Although Ellie was dying to find out all about the new girl, she was so excited to see her best friend again. "Hey, Grace!" She ran over and hugged her. "Isn't it great that we're sharing a room?" she cried.

"Brilliant!" Grace replied, grinning at Ellie. She dumped her bags onto her bed and then flopped down beside them. "It's so nice to be back," she sighed happily. And then she turned to Molly. "Hello," she said. "You must be Molly. I saw your name on the notice board. I'm Grace."

Ellie watched her friend chatting to the new girl. Grace looked really well, she thought with relief; quite a contrast to the tense, stressed-out Grace of last term. With a little shudder, Ellie remembered how unhappy and strangely behaved Grace had become. She'd been diagnosed as having a mild form of Obsessive-Compulsive Personality Disorder—or OCPD. It was thought that it might have been brought on by Grace having too much pressure from her mom, who always wanted Grace to be the best in class. Once her OCPD had been diagnosed, Grace had received counseling—and her mom had stopped pushing Grace so hard. So, hopefully, all that was now in the past.

"How come you're here?" Grace was asking Molly. "I hope that doesn't sound rude—I mean, how did you get a place here? Did you audition?"

"Well," Molly began, but before she could say another word, the door opened again and in walked Bryony.

"Bryony!" Ellie and Grace cried happily, running over to see her.

"How was your summer?"

"Good to see you!"

"Come and meet Molly!" they said together, the words rushing out before Bryony had a chance to reply.

Bryony looked a little taken aback, but Molly just smiled cheerfully at her. "Hi . . . er, Molly," Bryony said, her eyes wide. "Are you going to be a student here?"

Ellie gave Bryony a little nudge. "Didn't you read to the end of the dorm list, Bryony?" she chided jokingly. "This is Molly Baker—she's taken Sophie's place."

Ellie felt Bryony stiffen in shock at her words, and felt a little bit bad. That had been a tactless way to say it, she realized. Bryony had been particularly close to Sophie.

But Bryony recovered herself quickly. "I'm Bryony," she said to Molly, with a faint smile.

"Nice to meet you, Bryony," Molly beamed at her. "Oh, and who's this?"

Ellie and her friends turned to see Lara and Kate coming into the dorm.

"Hi, guys!" Lara called. "Great to see you!" Her eyebrows went right up into her flame-red hair as she spotted Molly. "Oh, hello," she said. "You must be the Molly Baker I've just seen on the dorm list, right? I'm Lara and this is Kate."

"Hello, Lara," Molly said, her eyes twinkling. "Hello, Kate. Oh, I hope I'm going to remember everyone's name. You're going to think I'm so rude if I keep forgetting who everybody is."

"We didn't know anyone else was starting," Kate said, gazing at Molly with interest. "When did you get your place here? Oh, and hello, by the way. Sorry—*I'm* the rude one, interrogating you before I've even said hello!"

Molly laughed. "Well, I . . ." she began—but, once again, there was an interruption as their new housemother, Mrs. Parrish, put her head around the door.

Mrs. Parrish looked a bit younger and trendier than their previous housemother, Mrs. Hall, and she had short blond hair and bright blue eyes. "Hello, everyone," she said, smiling around at all the girls. "I'm Mrs. Parrish, if you didn't already know—your new housemother for this year."

"Hello," Ellie and her friends chorused, smiling back. Mrs. Parrish reminded Ellie of a little bird, with her bright, interested eyes and her quick movements.

"I'd like us all to have a get-together in the Slip," Mrs. Parrish went on, "just to remind you of a few school rules and to give you your new timetables. And, of course," she added, with a little nod at Molly, "so that you can all be introduced to Molly properly. So, I'll see you all there in fifteen minutes or so. See if you can get unpacked by then."

Lara and Kate went back to the Billiard Room dorm, and Ellie and her new roommates got on with their unpacking. It was amazing how creased her clothes had become in the few hours since she'd packed them, Ellie thought dolefully. She'd tried to pack so carefully this time, too! But hanging up her new ballet uniform in her Year 8 wardrobe still felt great. And wasn't it strange to think of her old wardrobe in the Year 7 dorm being full of some other girl's things now?

Bryony started telling everyone a long and very funny story about her family's holiday in Spain. Ellie flashed Molly a smile, hoping she didn't feel left out. But Molly seemed okay—she was getting on with her unpacking, listening to Bryony's story, and laughing good-naturedly with the others at all the funny points.

By the time Bryony had finished, it was almost time for Mrs. Parrish's meeting.

"Now, where's this Slip again?" Molly said, smiling her wide smile. "I've forgotten how to get there already!" she joked.

Ellie and Grace laughed.

"The Slip is the easy bit, Molly," Grace replied. "It's right through the door. Now you've just got the rest of the school to learn your way around!"

•   •   •   •

It was great to see the other Year 8 girls as they all gathered in the Slip—Holly and Alice, Megan, Scarlett, and Rebecca—oh, and there was Isabelle, bursting through the door with her expensive-looking cases.

"Hello, everyone," Isabelle said, her olive cheeks blushing a little as she realized she was the last Year 8 girl to arrive at school. "I am so late because I have been arguing with my mother the whole way here," she explained, rolling her huge brown eyes. The French girl put down her cases with a sigh. "That woman! I am despairing of her!" she declared dramatically.

Ellie grinned at Isabelle, who had a somewhat tempestuous love-hate relationship with her mother. Clearly today was not one of the "love" days.

Isabelle suddenly spotted the dorm list on the notice board and rushed over to it. "Oh! But which dorm am I in?" she asked.

"You're with me and Kate—on the west side of the Billiard Room," Lara called out to her.

Isabelle beamed. "That is *formidable!*" she said, breaking into French in her excitement.

"Welcome back, Isabelle," Mrs. Parrish said, coming into the room. "Do go and drop off those cases—could somebody help Isabelle, please? We will wait for you here."

Lara and Kate got up from where they'd been perched on the windowsill to help their dorm-mate, while Ellie and her friends squeezed onto the sofa together.

Once everybody was gathered again in the Slip, Mrs. Parrish started the meeting. "Welcome back to The Royal Ballet School, everyone," she began. "I'm looking forward to getting to know you all, and I'm sure you're going to have great fun in Year 8—as well as work very hard, too, of course," she added, with a twinkle in her blue eyes. "As you all will now have discovered, we have a new girl—Molly Baker."

"Hi, guys," Molly said, getting to her feet and dropping a neat little curtsy.

"I know you'll all make Molly feel very welcome here at

Lower School," Mrs. Parrish said with a smile. "And Molly, to save yourself having to repeat your life story eleven times over to the others, perhaps you could say a few words about yourself to the girls now?"

"Sure," Molly replied, looking around the room. "Well, I'm Molly, I'm twelve years old, and from Coventry, in the Midlands— yes, where Lady Godiva came from," she said with a roll of her eyes.

Ellie grinned. She had learned about Lady Godiva in one of her history lessons. Hundreds of years ago, Lady Godiva had ridden her horse through town, naked, in protest about high taxes!

"I only started ballet three years ago," Molly continued, "which I guess is quite late, compared with you guys. My best friend was desperate to do ballet and talked me into going with her. So I did." She paused and grinned around the room. "And, if I'm really honest, I wasn't that crazy about ballet at first—I just did it to keep my friend company. My teacher was really nice and told me she thought I had natural talent, but I thought, *Yeah, yeah, she's just saying that to keep up the numbers in her class!*"

Ellie chuckled, wondering what had changed Molly's mind about dancing. Something obviously had!

"Then, last Christmas, I went on a school trip to see the Birmingham Royal Ballet perform *Cinderella*," Molly went on. Her eyes went far away for a moment. "And I just *loved* it," she said passionately. "Truly loved it. I'd never seen anything so wonderful, so exciting, so completely beautiful . . ." She grinned a little self-consciously. "And, from then on, I was hooked! It was like a light went on in my head and . . ." She shrugged. "I think I knew from that point, I really wanted to make a go of dancing. It was like . . . I got it. You know?"

Ellie found herself nodding. Oh, she knew all right. She totally understood how Molly had felt. Ellie had been bitten by the ballet bug when she was just three. In her case, her grandma had taken her to see a performance of *The Nutcracker*—and she'd become immediately hooked. She'd been given a video of the ballet the following Christmas, and had driven her mom nuts asking to watch it again and again, trying to copy the steps. Like Molly, there had been no going back for Ellie.

"So, anyway, all of a sudden I was working like crazy in my ballet class," Molly went on. "And then, last term, my teacher called The Royal Ballet School because she thought I . . . well, she thought I was good enough, I suppose. She spoke to Ms. Purvis, the principal, who suggested I come and join a Year 7 class here one day so that she could watch me."

"But you didn't come to join in any of our classes last term," Lara pointed out, looking confused.

Molly shook her head. "It turned out that Ms. Purvis was so busy with the end-of-year performance, the only class she was free to sit in on was an afternoon class with the Year 8s," she explained. "So I joined in that one instead."

"Wow," Kate said out loud. "That must have been hard."

Molly shot her a grateful smile. "Thanks for saying that—it

was! It was really hard. Technically, most of it was way beyond me. And, of course, I was absolutely terrified!"

Ellie warmed to the new girl even more. Molly was so open and honest about her feelings.

"Anyway, to cut a long story short," Molly continued, "Ms. Purvis offered me a trial year to see if I can cope with The Royal Ballet School training, what with me being such a late starter. And so here I am—and I'm going to give it my absolute best shot!"

Mrs. Parrish was smiling. "What Molly didn't tell you—out of modesty, no doubt—was that Ms. Purvis was really impressed by Molly's potential," she added. "Molly wouldn't have been offered a trial year here if Ms. Purvis didn't think she had an excellent chance of meeting The Royal Ballet School standard."

Molly flushed a little at that and sat down quickly.

"Now, obviously, Molly will have a lot to catch up on," said Mrs. Parrish. "And I'm sure you all remember how daunting it is to start at The Royal Ballet School. So it would be great if everybody could make her feel welcome and help her settle in as quickly as possible."

Ellie found herself nodding. Absolutely! She was sure she was going to get along fine with Molly. And she couldn't wait to see her dance! Ellie herself had been dancing for eight years now—and most of her school friends had at least five or six years of ballet under their belts, too. How would Molly compare, when she'd only been dancing for three years?

"Moving on from Molly, if we may," Mrs. Parrish went on, "there are some other things to tell you about. I have copies of your new timetable here. Could somebody pass them around, please? We'll run through them together."

Ellie jumped up to hand the timetables around, and then sat down with her own copy, scanning it eagerly.

"You'll see that your classical ballet class is now at two o'clock every day instead of being first thing in the morning," Mrs. Parrish pointed out. "And this year, your weekly character class will be separate from the boys'," she added. "But you'll also be having a weekly Irish dancing class . . ."

"Hooray!" Lara cheered.

Ellie grinned at her Irish friend. No prizes for guessing who was going to be the star performer in *that* class!

"And Irish dancing is a mixed class, so you'll get to dance with the boys then instead," Mrs. Parrish told them. "What else? Oh yes . . ." She began running through the house rules. When she'd finished, she looked up at the clock. "I'd better call the meeting to a close now because it's almost time to get together with your school 'families' and meet the Year 7 students you will be guiding," she told them.

Ellie smiled at their new housemother's mention of the great "family" support system that operated for new students within The Royal Ballet Lower School. Each new student was assigned to an older student to whom they could turn for support and advice to help them settle in. As Year 8 students, Ellie and her friends would each be a "guide" to a new Year 7 student.

Ellie had been assigned as guide to a girl named Julia Banks. As was the school tradition, Ellie had decorated a pair of her old pointe shoes for Julia. She'd mailed them to her over the summer vacation, along with a friendly letter introducing herself and promising Julia that she was going to love Lower School! Ellie's own guide, Jessica, who was now in Year 9, had done the same thing for Ellie the year before, and Ellie had treasured her letter that whole summer, reading it over and over again.

"The only exception is Molly, of course," Mrs. Parrish went on, turning to the new girl. "Being new yourself, Molly, we obviously won't expect you to guide one of the Year 7s. You'll be meeting your own guide instead, today."

"Phew, thank goodness for that," Molly said with a grin.

"Grace, would you make sure that Molly knows where she's going, please?" Mrs. Parrish asked.

Grace nodded and smiled at Molly.

Mrs. Parrish then stood up. "I'll be around all day today if anyone needs to speak to me about anything else," she finished. "So . . . off you go, and I shall see you all later."

Ellie got up from the sofa, feeling excited about meeting Julia—and looking forward to seeing Jessica again, of course. Julia was the younger sister of Sarah Banks, who had been Grace's guide. *Lower School really is like one big, interconnected family*, she thought happily as she followed her friends out of the Slip. *And I'm so glad to be a part of it!*

•　　•　　•　　•

Ellie and the others arrived in the assembly hall to find the new Year 7 students clustered together, whispering nervously to one another. She went over to join Jessica, and then Mrs. Hall began reading out the names of the Year 7 girls one by one. As she did so, each girl stepped forward and was then joined by her guide and her guide's guide—her Royal Ballet School "family."

When Mrs. Hall called out, "Julia Banks," a small, blond girl stepped forward.

Ellie waved. "Over here, Julia!" she called. She and Jessica began to walk toward her, and a tentative smile passed over the new girl's face.

"Hi!" Ellie said brightly. "I'm Ellie, your guide." She reached out to give her new charge a hug, and felt really grown-up all of a sudden.

"Thank you," Julia said shyly, her cheeks turning pink.

"And this is Jessica, who's *my* guide," Ellie went on.

"Hi, Julia," Jessica said, leaning forward to hug Julia, too. "I know your sister, Sarah. I'm sure she's told you loads of useful stuff about Lower School, but we're here for you, as well, if you need to know anything else—or if you just want a chat."

Julia looked up at Jessica and went even pinker. "Thank you," she said again.

"And please don't look so worried," Ellie said reassuringly. "I was feeling just like you are this time last year—nervous about all the new names and faces I had to get to know, as well as a new school to find my way around. But I promise you, you'll settle in really fast. Lower School is a great place to be! You'll love it here."

Julia seemed to relax a little then, and this time she smiled like she meant it. "I think I already do," she said.

Dear Diary,

Well, the new term has begun—and it's already shaping up to be a good one! It is kind of weird, though, being in a small dorm after last year—and even weirder not having Sophie around. But it's great to be back, and I can't wait to get into my ballet things and dance again tomorrow.

Better go—I want to catch up with the others a bit more, and get to know Molly better, before Mrs. Parrish comes around to say that it's lights-out!

Chapter 2

Being a Year 8 girl was definitely going to take a bit of getting used to, Ellie decided the following morning. As a Year 7 student, she had started every school day with ballet class straight after breakfast—which was a pretty good way to ensure she always woke up feeling excited. Now, things would be different. Ballet was in the afternoons for this school year—between two and four o'clock. Instead of dancing all morning, Ellie had three academic lessons to sit through!

But at least the week started with a subject she liked—English. Ms. Swaisland, their teacher, got everybody thinking by giving them a creative writing assignment entitled "Disaster Strikes!"

"Let's begin work on this as a group, to get you thinking," she said, chalking the title up on the blackboard. "Any suggestions? It can be anything from a huge natural disaster—like an earthquake, flood, or tornado—to a tiny, more domestic disaster like . . . losing your lucky mascot, or chipping your nail varnish . . ." She held up her hands and pulled a comic expression, making everybody laugh. "The important thing is to draw me into it," she urged them. "Make what I'm reading matter to me. Make me suffer!"

"Disaster Strikes! I've lost my pen!" Ellie heard her friend Matt Haslum say in a low voice.

Ms. Swaisland heard it, too, and raised her eyebrows. "I'm not suffering yet, Matt," she said. "Give me some drama!"

"No, I really *have* lost my pen," Matt replied sheepishly. He began rummaging around in his pencil tin.

Ms. Swaisland smiled. "Okay, somebody else give me a truly dramatic reason why Matt losing his pen could really be a disaster," she shot back. "Use your imagination!"

Alice put up her hand. "His pen is a family heirloom, handed down to him by his great-great-great-grandfather, who happened to be an . . . um . . . emperor of a far-off land," she improvised.

"Wow," Matt said. "It *is* just a Biro, though . . ."

Ms. Swaisland nodded. "Good, Alice! I like it! Anybody else?"

Luke Bailey, the boy sitting next to Matt, put up his hand. "The pen is actually a secret camera, used for detective work. Matt's not really a ballet student—he's a spy sent here to find out our darkest secrets. Without his pen, he'll lose his job—and probably be tortured to death!"

Matt gave Luke a friendly punch on the arm. "Cheers, mate," he said.

Ms. Swaisland opened her eyes wide, pretending to be horrified. "Nice idea, Luke!" She looked around the class again. "Any other reasons why Matt losing his pen could be a real disaster?" she asked.

With a giggle Grace, put her hand up. "He won't be able to

do any work, Ms. Swaisland—and then he'll get into big trouble from you!"

"You've all got it in for me today," Matt complained, although Ellie could see that he really thought it was funny, too.

Ms. Swaisland took her own pen and gave it to Matt. "Well, we certainly don't want that to happen," she said with a twinkle in her eye. "Here, Matt, borrow this for the rest of the lesson. So that's your assignment, which I'd like in two weeks' time, please . . ."

•   •   •   •

Chemistry came next. Not one of Ellie's favorite subjects, but their teacher, Dr. Warburton, was very jolly and friendly, and she set them some fun experiments to do in pairs.

Then came drama. Their teacher, Mr. Barrington, asked the boys to become old women, and the girls to become old men. Then he asked them to dance in their new guises. Ellie couldn't stop giggling as she and her friends stiffly went through a couple of *pliés*, clutching their backs and complaining as they did so.

Molly made everyone laugh by being an old man trying to do really funky dance moves. "I'm ninety-eight, but I still go clubbing every weekend," she quavered, pretending to boogie around a walking stick. Ellie thought she was about to cry with laughter at Molly's performance. Clowning around like that, stealing the show, the new girl reminded Ellie of Sophie.

And then after lunch it was, at last, time to get changed for their first Year 8 ballet class!

"Looking on the bright side," Grace said as they made their

way into the Room Off, "though we don't start the day with ballet anymore, at least our afternoons are going to be heavenly!"

"You're right," Ellie agreed. "And, actually, our regular school lessons this morning were quite fun, on the whole."

"The teachers are softening us up in this first week of term," Bryony joked, beginning to brush out her long black hair. "Next week, the hard work will kick in—you wait!"

"Most girls our age have regular lessons all day—and no ballet whatsoever," Molly reminded them with a smile. She lifted her new ballet uniform from her wardrobe and gazed at it lovingly. "And that would have been me today, at my old school. But here I am, getting ready to dance. I'm sooo lucky!" She grinned at the others. "I can take working a bit harder in the mornings if it makes time for ballet in the afternoons!"

Ellie smiled and nodded as she pulled on her blue leotard over her new pink tights. She gazed at her reflection in the full-length mirror that hung in the dorm. "You know, I got so used to seeing Jessica and the rest of her class in this cornflower blue last year, it feels weird to see myself in it now. I feel a bit like an impostor!" she joked.

"And Jessica is probably saying to herself how weird it is to be dancing in maroon, the Year 9 color," Grace observed.

Molly was looking a little confused, so Ellie quickly explained. "At The Royal Ballet School, the girls wear a different color leotard each year. Here, at Lower School, the Year 7s wear pink, the Year 8s cornflower blue, the Year 9s maroon, the Year 10s royal blue, and the Year 11s lilac."

"And then, at Upper School, the 1st Years wear pale blue, the 2nd Years wear royal blue, and the 3rd Year Graduates wear burgundy," Grace put in.

"What about the boys?" Molly asked, wide-eyed. "Do they change their uniforms every year, too?"

Ellie nodded, and began to reel off the boys' ballet uniforms. "Let's see . . . Year 7s wear royal blue singlets and black shorts . . . Year 8s wear royal blue singlets and matching footless tights . . . Year 9s wear white singlets with gray tights . . . Year 10s wear white singlets with navy tights . . . and Year 11s wear white singlets with black tights," she finished. She smoothed out her leotard and then turned to Molly. "I think we girls get a much better deal in the color department!" she added with a grin.

Molly nodded. "You know, I'm really looking forward to seeing the boys dance," she said. "There weren't *any* boys in my old ballet class in Coventry. All the boys I knew would rather have bitten off their own arms than put on a pair of ballet shoes and jump around."

"Well you won't have long to wait," Grace told her. "We'll get to do Irish dancing classes with them every week, so you can see them in action then."

Ellie glanced over at Bryony, who was being very quiet, she noticed. "Are you all right, Bryony?" she asked curiously.

"Well . . . it's just a bit weird, this, isn't it?" Bryony burst out suddenly. "I mean, getting ready for ballet like this, without the rest of the girls. It doesn't feel right." Bryony paused and then went on. "No offense to you guys, but . . . I don't know if I'm going to like being in such a small dorm," she admitted. "I miss all the others. But especially Sophie . . ." Her voice trailed away, leaving an uncomfortable silence.

Ellie glanced at Molly, concerned she might feel a little left out of the conversation, never having met Sophie. "I think its cozy in here," she said quickly. "And I certainly didn't miss Lara snoring last night!" she joked. "Or that noisy clock of Isabelle's ticktocking so annoyingly . . ."

"True!" Grace agreed fervently as she coated her bun in hairspray. "I like it being just the four of us."

Ellie gulped as she caught sight of her watch. "Oops! What I *am* missing, though, is Megan telling us it's time to go to class already!" she said, hurriedly grabbing her water bottle. "Come on, guys—or we'll be late!"

Ellie and the others rushed out of their room—heck, all the Billiard Room girls had left already!—and down the corridor toward their ballet studio. Ellie's heart was thumping with excitement. She couldn't wait to meet their new teacher, Ms. Black, and to feel her body stretching out in all the familiar ballet poses once more.

In the studio, the rest of the girls from their year were already limbering up at the barre; a sea of cornflower blue. No sign of Ms. Black yet, though—phew! At least she wasn't there to see Ellie and her friends tumbling into the studio last of all!

Ellie quickly peeled off her red sweat suit and put on her ballet shoes. "Leave your things at the side of the studio," she told Molly, "and then come and start warming up at the barre with us, before Ms. Black gets here."

"Thanks," Molly said gratefully. "All of a sudden I feel really nervous about this!"

"Once you start dancing, your body will take over and you'll feel better, I'm certain," Ellie reassured her.

"Thanks," Molly said. "I hope so!"

Ellie hummed to herself as she stretched out her muscles at the barre alongside Grace, with Molly on the other side, and her heart slowed to a regular beat as she gradually relaxed. Oh, it was lovely to be back at school. And it was *wonderful* to be back in the studio!

"Good afternoon, girls," came a voice just then, and Ellie abandoned her warm-up *pliés* at once. Ms. Black had arrived!

Ellie turned—just like every other girl in the room—to see the new teacher. Ellie's mouth felt dry. She'd loved being taught by Ms. Wells last year. She so hoped she was going to feel the same way about Ms. Black. "Good afternoon," she replied in a chorus with the other girls.

Ms. Black was petite and Mediterranean-looking, with olive skin, and dark curly hair that was piled up on top of her head with a clip. Her smile was wide and friendly as she gazed around the room at her new students. "Hello, everyone! I'm Ms. Black, if you hadn't already guessed," she said, in a warm, clear voice. "Perhaps we could go around the room, with each of you telling me your name?" She gestured toward Lara, who stood at one end of the long barre that lined three sides of the studio.

"Lara McCloud," Lara began, bobbing a little curtsy.

Ms. Black smiled and nodded.

"Isabelle Armand," said Isabelle, who was next, dropping into a far deeper and more lavish curtsy than Lara's.

Ellie grinned. Trust flamboyant Isabelle to go all out to impress their new teacher as soon as she could!

Ms. Black nodded and smiled. "Next?" she said, looking at Kate.

Kate gave a curtsey. "Kate Walker," she said quietly.

Ms. Black's eyes narrowed in recognition of the name. Ellie was quite sure their teacher must already know that Kate Walker was the daughter of Lim Soo May and Christopher Bell, two world-famous dancers. But Ms. Black just nodded and smiled again before moving on, without making any comment. Ellie knew that Kate would be relieved at that. Her friend dreaded being judged by her parents' standards, or being compared with them in any way.

The girls went around introducing themselves. Grace was before Ellie, and she blushed bright red as she dropped a perfect curtsy. Ms. Black gave Grace a warm smile—and Ellie wondered if she knew that Grace had had doubts about staying at The Royal Ballet School. But before she could dwell on that, it was her own turn.

Ellie took a deep breath and curtsied as prettily as she could. "Ellie Brown," she said, smiling at Ms. Black.

Ms. Black returned the smile, her dark eyes twinkling.

"Molly Baker," Molly then said, with a dimply grin. She dropped a graceful, seemingly effortless curtsy. "Also known around here as the New Girl," she added.

Ms. Black laughed. "Welcome, Molly, I'm sure you'll soon settle in," she said.

Finally, Bryony, the last girl in the line, curtsied and introduced herself.

"And now that we all know one another," Ms. Black said, "you'd better show me what you are capable of." She flashed them another smile. "So let's begin."

Ellie felt jittery as she went back to the barre. Glancing at Grace's tense face to her left, Ellie guessed that she was feeling the same way. Molly, on her right, looked even more apprehensive. Not only would she have the teacher assessing her performance, she would no doubt have the rest of the class checking her out, too, wondering how the new girl would measure up. *Talk about pressure!* thought Ellie, wincing in sympathy.

"Don't worry—I know your bodies will be a little out of shape after the summer break," Ms. Black added reassuringly. "I'm not expecting you to be back at full strength and flexibility straightaway. It will take a week or so."

Ellie felt a little rush of relief. Having had several weeks away from rigorous daily ballet classes, she'd been secretly concerned about being stiff and out of condition. She was pleased that Ms. Black was going to ease them in gently. She really wanted to make a good first impression on her new teacher!

"So for this first week, we'll be reconditioning your bodies—which I'm afraid is a rather slow, and sometimes painful, period," Ms. Black explained. She came into the center of the studio. "Facing the barre then, please, and we'll get those feet warmed up and stretching."

There was a rustle of movement as Ellie and the other girls turned to face the barre and prepare for the exercise.

"Working the leg in a circle, please—we'll do this *en dehors* first of all—away from your supporting leg. So . . . start in first position, *dégagé devant,* letting the working foot really feel the floor as you point forward, rotate to second position, feeling the turn out in the hip, flex the foot up, and stretch again to *pointe tendu,* keeping the leg stretched rotate to *derierre* close back into first position and *demi-plié,* soft easy bend of the knees, repeat with the other foot," Ms. Black reminded them, watching as the girls performed the movement. "That's it. Twice on each leg, please, then repeat *en dedans,* toward the supporting leg."

As Ellie turned out her leg from the hip joint in the familiar *rond de jambe à terre,* she watched herself in the mirror. There she was, all in blue, like a true Year 8 girl, back in the ballet studio at Lower School. *Heaven,* she thought with a small smile.

She finished working her right leg and repeated the exercise *en dedans.* And even though she knew she should try to stay absolutely focused on what her own body was doing, Ellie just couldn't help sneaking glances at how the new girl was doing.

You can't really judge someone on the barre exercises alone, Ellie thought as she watched Molly work through the movements, *but it's obvious even from those that she has something.* The new girl certainly had natural grace—although it was also obvious to Ellie straight away that her technique needed work.

Ms. Black had spotted this, too, of course. She came over to adjust Molly's body. Ellie had found it strange being "adjusted" like a shop mannequin at first, but now she was quite used to it, and appreciated any extra attention the teachers gave her.

Molly, however, seemed to be a little unsettled by this. As Ms. Black moved Molly's arm into the correct position, then turned her leg out from the hip joint a fraction more, Molly seemed to flush with embarrassment. Ellie hastily looked away, not wanting the new girl to feel under even more scrutiny.

Surely Molly's old ballet teacher must have done the same, though? Ellie reasoned to herself. *So maybe she's just embarrassed because she's the first one in class to be singled out for correction.*

Ms. Black took the girls through a whole series of barre exercises, several *port de bras* exercises for their arms, and then asked them to move into the center of the studio.

"As it is your first ballet class of the term, we'll have a nice, easy *adage*—not too slow," she said with a smile. "So, standing in fifth position . . ." Ms. Black took the position herself, and then, calling out the moves as she went, demonstrated the *adage* she wanted the class to perform. "*Croisé chassé* forward, and lift into *attitude* . . . extend the leg and arms to first *arabesque* . . . *fondu* on supporting leg . . . and *pas de bourrée* to face the other corner . . . rise onto *demi-pointe* and lower . . . and repeat on other leg," she finished.

Along with the other girls, Ellie performed the *adage* movements as diligently as she could—but, boy, was she feeling rusty! Ms. Black came over to correct her *chassé,* and she wobbled horribly when they were all doing their *attitudes. Oh, dear!* Ellie thought glumly. She hoped Ms. Black wasn't writing her off already. Her body didn't feel anything like as flexible as it had done six weeks ago.

Molly seemed even more wobbly, Ellie noticed. She got the order of the steps wrong a couple of times, and was very shaky in her *arabesques* too.

Several of the other girls were also checking out the new girl. Most looked sympathetic. But not Bryony, Ellie couldn't help noticing. The frown on Bryony's face when she glanced at Molly made it quite plain: She didn't think much of Molly's dancing.

By the end of class, everyone seemed a little relieved that it was over.

"My *arabesque*—pah! I was shocked at my own badness," Isabelle groaned, with feeling. "I was like a robot—all stiff and mechanical. No . . . how do you say it? No *flow.*"

"No flow for me, either," Lara said, rubbing her damp face with a towel. "I was awful! Ms. Black must think I'm a complete dunce."

"Me too," Ellie said, pulling on her sweatpants. She couldn't help but feel a little disappointed in the way she'd performed. It was kind of an anticlimax. She'd dreamed for so long about being back in the studio again and dancing gloriously, but now . . . now she just hoped she got back up to speed, fast. She hated feeling so leaden and stiff!

"How about you, Molly?" she asked, remembering the new girl. "It must be a bit of a relief to have gotten through the first class in one piece."

Molly smiled and nodded. "I'm so sweaty . . . and tired . . . and achey!" She laughed. "And I know I'm going to pay for this tomorrow. I think my muscles will seize up overnight!" She smoothed her hair away from her face. "I loved it, though," she added, her eyes shining. "Even though I feel a bit daunted now by how good everyone else is—"

"Good?" Isabelle interrupted with a snort. "You are too kind, I think, Molly!"

Ellie grinned. Isabelle, like all the other Royal Ballet School students, just hated feeling that they hadn't danced the best they could. "Come on," Ellie said. "We'll all feel better after tuck. I have a whole new bag of gummy bears that I'm planning to make a dent in."

•   •   •   •

Later, up in the dorm, Ellie and Bryony were first out of the showers.

"So, what did you think?" Bryony asked in a low voice.

"What did I think of what?" Ellie replied, as she pulled on a sweatshirt and pair of jeans.

"Of Molly, in ballet," Bryony said, glancing furtively in the direction of the bathroom.

"She was okay, I guess," Ellie replied. Then, because she felt deceitful talking about the new girl behind her back, she added, "I didn't really get to see much of her. I was too busy worrying about my own tired body to notice."

"Well, I checked her out," Bryony said. "And I'm not being funny, but Sophie was definitely a better dancer than she is. And if that's the case, then I don't think it's fair that—"

Molly and Grace came back into the dorm just then, toweling their hair, and Bryony broke off. A guilty flush spread over her cheeks, and she buttoned up her school blouse in silence.

"You were right, Ellie," Molly said, rummaging in her wardrobe for her school uniform. "I feel so much better after that. That lovely hot shower has almost made me forget how hard that ballet class was."

Bryony looked pointedly at Ellie, at Molly's words. *See?* she seemed to be saying. *She can't cut it!*

Ellie looked away from Bryony and smiled at Molly. "I found it hard, too," she said deliberately. "But we'll all be better tomorrow, I'm sure." It was unfair to compare Molly with Sophie right now, she thought privately. Bryony wasn't giving Molly much of a chance to prove herself. After all, The Royal Ballet School was giving Molly a whole year to catch up and prove that she was good enough to stay.

•   •   •   •

Ellie felt ravenous as she queued with her friends to collect their tuck boxes full of goodies. She hadn't done such a long stint of intensive ballet all summer—and her body was telling her it needed refueling, and fast! She was starting to feel better about the class now. At least everyone else had found it hard, too; nobody seemed to think they'd danced particularly well. Ellie could comfort herself with the fact that she probably hadn't stuck out to Ms. Black as the only one struggling!

"Hey, Ellie!" came a familiar voice just then.

Ellie turned to see Matt coming up to join the end of the queue, with Luke close behind him. "Hi Matt, hi Luke," she said, smiling. Ellie and Matt were old buddies, having been dance partners back when they were JAs—Junior Associates of The Royal Ballet School—before they'd even started at Lower School. Ellie hadn't seen Matt hang out with Luke Bailey much before—but like the girls, the boys had been split into smaller dorms this year, and Ellie had heard that Matt was now sharing a dorm with Luke and two of the other boys, Danny Bourne and Justin Vafadari.

"So how was ballet for you guys?" she asked. "The girls are all feeling pretty beat, I can tell you!"

"Ditto for the guys," Matt replied. "I feel like I've gone under a steamroller now, I'm so stretched out."

"Our new teacher's a bit of a slave driver," Luke said with a

"She seemed really nice," Ellie said. "I just hated feeling so rusty in front of her, though. You know? Like I wouldn't have minded Ms. Wells seeing me like that because she knew I could do better than that, but for a new teacher, you want to look your best, don't you?"

"You always look great to me, Ellie." Luke smiled, helping himself to a cold drink from the chiller cabinet.

Ellie felt herself blush. "Oh, well . . ." she said, feeling a little awkward.

Matt elbowed Luke. "Hey, smooth talker!" he said. "You've embarrassed Ellie now."

Ellie managed to regain her composure and grin at Luke. "No worries," she said. "You can compliment me anytime you like, Luke!" As he smiled back, Ellie was struck by the blueness of his eyes. She realized she was staring rather blatantly at him, and quickly dragged her gaze away.

The two boys drifted over to sit down with their tuck boxes, and Lara turned to Ellie. "I like Luke's new haircut," she said. "It's really cool, isn't it? He seems really tall, as well," she added. "He must have had a growth spurt over the summer! I bet he's the tallest boy in class now."

Ellie nodded, glad for an excuse to look at Luke again. She felt as if she'd never really looked at him before. It was very strange. How could she not have noticed how good-looking he was? She hadn't had much to do with Luke last year. Matt had been her closest buddy of the boys. She dragged her eyes away in case Luke turned and caught her staring again. She realized that her face felt hot. Goodness! What was happening? Why did she have such a fluttery feeling starting up inside her?

You always look great to me, Ellie . . . he'd said to her. The thought of his words made her feel all shivery inside.

"Ellie? Ellie!" Grace said, elbowing her. "You're next! Ellie! Do you want anything to drink or not?"

Ellie blushed scarlet. "Um . . . yes," she said. "Just thinking about something."

"Well, think about tuck instead," Grace laughed. "Or we'll still be here at lights-out!"

●　　　●　　　●　　　●

That evening, Ellie went to the common room with some of the other girls. That much hadn't changed, at least; as Year 8s they'd had the same common room as last year. It was strange, though, to see the new Year 7s in there. Jessica and her gang had now moved on to the Year 9 and Year 10 girls' common room.

The newcomers all looked exhausted after their first full day at Lower School, but were all chattering excitedly, and asking the older girls all sorts of questions about life there.

Ellie was pleased to see that Julia seemed to have hooked up with a couple of girls and was looking quite at home on one of the huge, plum-colored sofas.

"So are we allowed to have midnight feasts?" a red-haired girl named Emma asked excitedly. A few of her friends giggled. "But that's what everyone does at boarding school, isn't it?" said Emma indignantly.

"We did have a midnight feast last year," Ellie told them, with a grin.

"But we got caught!" Lara added.

"Mrs. Hall was really mad with us," Grace told the new girls.

"Do you remember Sophie's ghost story, though?" Bryony asked, her eyes shining. "She was sooo good at that kind of stuff. She scared everyone to death, didn't she? Do you remember the way we all screamed at the end of it?"

Molly was looking a little lost at the direction the conversation had taken—as were the Year 7 girls—so Ellie explained. "Sophie was in our class last year. And at the midnight feast she told us a ghost story—which got spookier and spookier—and at the end, she really made us all jump, and everyone started screaming their heads off."

"Which woke up half the school—*and* our housemother!" Grace added.

"We got into so much trouble!" laughed Lara. She smiled at the Year 7s. "So if you're planning a midnight feast, no ghost stories allowed!"

"What happened to your friend Sophie?" Emma wanted to know.

"She was assessed out," Lara said quietly.

"She's at a performing arts school in Manchester now," Ellie added, "and so far, she's really loving it there. So there *is* a happy ending."

"It's not the same here without Soph, though," Bryony said, her eyes far away.

"Sure, she was great to have around," Lara agreed. She turned her gaze to the Year 7s. "But before you all start worrying, it's really rare for anyone to get assessed out in Year 7. So it's not likely to happen to any of you guys, okay?"

"Thanks," said a wide-eyed blonde girl called Rose. "I was just starting to panic already!"

"Do you keep in touch with Sophie much?" Molly asked Bryony chattily.

"Loads," Bryony replied. "We spoke on the phone most weeks over the summer, and send each other lots of e-mails." Then she turned away from Molly to address the other Year 8 girls. "Hey, do you remember that awful fortune-telling game Soph had last term?" she asked them. "What was the prediction she gave you again, Lara?"

Ellie felt a little taken aback. Was Bryony deliberately snubbing Molly? She turned to Molly herself, not even sure what she was going to say, just wanting to make the new girl feel included.

But Molly had already gotten to her feet and was making her way to the door. "I think I'm going to give my mum a call," she said quietly. "See you all later."

Dear Diary,

I'm writing this in bed, quickly, before Mrs. Parrish comes around to tell us that it's lights-out time. Molly's already asleep—and I feel pretty tired, too. My whole body aches from our first ballet class—it really felt like a punishing workout, building up my stamina and strength again. I hope it doesn't take long for me to get back to form.

Bryony was acting a bit strangely tonight. Not exactly rude to Molly . . . but not exactly welcoming, either. I don't know if everybody else noticed she was being a bit cool, but I'm pretty sure Molly picked up on it. What's all this about? It's just not like Bryony to be so unfriendly.

Better sign off—I can hear Mrs. Parrish's footsteps . . . I wonder what I'll dream about tonight? Adage or pirouettes—or maybe Luke Bailey . . . ! He said something really nice to me today. And now he keeps popping into my head!

Chapter 3

"And this morning, ladies, we have French, IT, and math," Grace read aloud from her class schedule the next day.

"No! My three worst subjects, one after the other!" Molly said, slipping her arms into her dressing gown with a yawn. "Ouch! My arms feel like tired bits of old string!"

"Maybe you could write your 'Disaster Strikes!' English assignment about Tuesday mornings," Ellie suggested with a grin.

Molly wriggled her shoulder blades and winced. "Good idea! My whole body feels like a disaster after yesterday's ballet class!" she confessed.

"Does it?" Bryony asked curiously.

Molly turned a bit red. "Oh, no—don't tell me you all feel okay? Am I the only one suffering here?" she asked.

Bryony shrugged. "I feel fine," she said, picking up her towel and wash bag. She turned and made her way out toward the bathroom.

"Don't worry, Molly," Grace said comfortingly. "My arms and legs are pretty achey, too."

"And mine," Ellie added. "I'm sure they will be for the next few days, but we'll all get used to it—eventually!"

Molly laughed, but didn't look too sure. "I hope so," she said with a grin as she pretended to hobble out toward the bathroom. "I keep telling myself 'no pain, no gain,' but right now, I think I'd just settle for 'no pain'!"

●   ●   ●   ●

Over breakfast, Ellie found herself staring at Luke again as he took a tray and helped himself to breakfast while laughing and joking with Matt. *Stop it, Ellie!* she told herself, and gazed fiercely into her cereal bowl instead.

"Something wrong with your breakfast, Ellie?" Molly asked.

Ellie realized her nose was now practically touching her bowl. She lifted her head and grinned sheepishly. "No," she replied. "I was just . . . um . . ."

"Are these seats free?" came Matt's voice from across the table.

Ellie looked across to see him and Luke hovering at the empty seats opposite her. "Oh! Yes!" she said. "Hiya, Matt. Hi, Luke." She felt her cheeks turn even hotter, and she busied herself stirring her porridge as if it were the most important thing in the world.

"Ellie! You're splashing me!" Grace complained as a fleck of porridge landed on her hand.

"Oh! Sorry, Grace . . ." Ellie muttered, and stopped her frantic stirring.

Luke grinned at her. "Lumpy porridge today, eh?" he asked.

"Something like that," Ellie said, smiling faintly in return.

"Well, it's very kind of you to want to share it, Ell, but I don't want any more, thanks," Grace joked as she wiped her hand clean.

"Sorry, Grace," Ellie said again. "Maybe I should just . . . eat it."

Get a hold of yourself, Ellie Brown! she told herself, spooning in a mouthful of porridge. *It's just silly getting all flustered because Luke Bailey is around!*

She tried to focus on what Megan was saying farther down the table, in the hope that it would take her mind off Luke.

"My sister says that all the boys in her class have the hots for Ms. Blanchard," she said, spreading honey on her toast. "And they especially love it when she reads aloud in French."

"Well, that is no surprise," said Isabelle with a casual shrug. "Maybe I am a little biased, being French myself, but no language in the world sounds so beautiful."

Matt laughed loudly. "Isabelle Armand, I just knew you were going to say that," he said teasingly. "According to you, the French are the best at everything!"

Isabelle smiled back. "Oh no, not *everything*, Matt," she said sweetly. "I think you English are better at . . . losing at football, *non?*"

"Oho! Fighting talk . . ." Luke said with a big grin. "What'll it be, then? *Baguettes* at dawn?"

Ellie giggled at his joke—a bit too loudly. The others looked at her curiously. Ellie felt herself going bright red again, and got to her feet abruptly. "Okay, I'm off to get my books," she said, grabbing her tray and breakfast things.

"Oh," Grace said. "Can't you wait a minute for me? I've nearly finished."

"Um . . . I've just remembered something I have to do in the dorm," Ellie improvised quickly. She just wanted to get out of the canteen now, before she made even more of a fool of herself in front of Luke. "I'll see you up there!"

She disposed of her tray and then made her way back up to the dorm, her cheeks still feeling fiery red. She had looked like a tomato in front of Luke Bailey! She hadn't even been able to get a proper sentence out! And as for that performance with her porridge . . . ! How embarrassing! She was acting like a loon. A love-struck loon!

The words hit her with such a shock that she froze on the spot in the corridor. Love-struck? Did she *really* have a crush on Luke Bailey?

•　　　•　　　•　　　•

During their first class, French, Ellie found it almost impossible to concentrate on what Ms. Blanchard was telling them about reflexive verbs. Luke Bailey was sitting in front of her, and where his hair had been cut short there was a little white line of skin that contrasted with the rest of his tan. For some reason, Ellie's eyes kept being drawn back to it. There was something so deeply cute about it! It was like a secret that only she had spotted.

In IT, the students were paired up to begin a website design project. Mrs. Sanderson paired Ellie with Molly, and the two girls spent ages trying to decide on a theme for their website.

"How about a fake pop band site?" Molly suggested. "We could do a fan-site for a made-up band or a celebrity or something . . ."

"A really *awful* celebrity," Ellie said, warming to the idea, "like a failed magician or something."

"Or someone who owns a TV star dog . . ." Molly giggled. "You know, one of those dogs you see in dog-food adverts."

"Or," Ellie said, having a brainwave, "we could do a site for girls like us, with loads of quizzes and personality tests and jokes . . ."

"Nice idea!" Molly agreed. "And we could have a gossip section, too," she added, "and puzzles. And horoscopes!"

The girls started work, and had great fun putting together a "Ballet Brainbusters" quiz. They were amazed when the bell rang to say that class was over.

"I can't believe I'm enjoying this morning so much," Molly said, backing up their quiz onto a CD and switching off the computer. "Surely I'm not going to like math here, too? I mean, that truly would be some kind of miracle."

Ellie laughed. She'd so enjoyed the IT class herself that she'd almost forgotten Luke was nearby, she realized. Now *that*, she reckoned, really *was* a miracle! But she certainly wasn't going to say anything about that!

•   •   •   •

While they were getting changed for their afternoon ballet class, Molly waved a printout of the quiz around the dorm. "Grace, Bryony—do either of you want to have a go at our ballet quiz later?" she asked. "Ellie and I did it for our website in IT."

"Count me in," Grace said at once as she stepped out of her school skirt. "I love quizzes like that."

"How about you, Bryony?" Molly asked again, with a smile.

Bryony was wetting her hair in front of the mirror to make it lie smooth. "No thanks," she said in a bored-sounding voice.

Molly looked a little taken aback, so Ellie quickly filled the silence. "Right, just Grace, then. Fire away with the first killer question then, Moll!"

Bryony switched on her hairdryer just as Molly opened her mouth to speak. "Sorry!" Bryony shouted above the whirr. "I've just got to dry this a bit—I put too much water on."

Molly put the quiz printout down and carried on getting ready for ballet class.

"There's not really time to do it now," she said quietly when Bryony finally switched off the hairdryer. "Maybe later."

Ellie tried to pretend nothing was wrong, but inside she felt a bit bad for the new girl. Molly was so nice and funny and friendly—why wasn't Bryony being more welcoming to her? Bryony was usually so cheerful and easygoing. She seemed to be really out of sorts since she'd arrived back at school.

●　　　●　　　●　　　●

That evening, in the common room, Bryony seemed particularly quiet and withdrawn.

"Is everything all right, Bry?" Ellie asked her.

Bryony gave a little shrug. "I had an e-mail from Sophie. I guess I'm just missing her, that's all," she said.

"How's she getting on?" asked Grace at once.

"Did you print it out?" Lara chimed in.

Bryony nodded, then took a crumpled piece of paper out of her pocket. She began to read it aloud.

"Hi there, Bry!

"Hope you're okay and that school is good. I'm just LOVING performing arts school! Keep having to stop myself from getting up on the table in the canteen and belting out 'Fame'! I've already made a really good friend—Tess—who is fab. You'd really like her. She has me in stitches the whole time with her jokes, and she acts the socks off me in drama. Some of the other girls here—Harriet and Nina and Lucy—seem great, too. Think I'm going to get along just fine—especially as the Christmas production this year is going to be *Grease!* I am trying out for every Pink Lady there is, of course!!

"How is everyone and everything at school? Say hi to the girls for me. I still read all your horoscopes in my magazines every week and think of you all. Write soon, anyway, with all the news.

"Loads of love and air-kisses (DAH-ling!!)

"Soph xxx"

Ellie felt herself smiling. It was almost as if Sophie had been in the room with them, her voice had come across so strong.

"I can just see Sophie as a Pink Lady," Lara laughed. "Nothing changes, eh?"

"Well, some things do change," Bryony said as she folded up the e-mail and put it back in her pocket. Her eyes flicked across at Molly. "Unfortunately . . ."

Ellie drew in a breath. She hoped that none of the others had noticed Bryony's apparent dig at the new girl. Especially Molly herself.

Some of the Year 7 girls came in then. Julia went over to switch on the television. "No one minds, do they?" she asked tentatively. "It's my favorite soap, and I can't bear to miss it . . ."

"Ours too," Ellie said quickly. She smiled at Julia, glad that the awkward moment had passed, but still feeling deeply uncomfortable about it. Had Bryony really meant to be that rude to Molly? Or was Ellie just reading too much into everything?

•   •   •   •

Bryony remained subdued all evening, and after lights-out Ellie decided to lighten the mood a bit. "G'night, Graycee," she said in an exaggerated Texas drawl.

Grace laughed. "There's an impostor in Ellie's bed!" she hissed to the others. And then she replied in a deep, growly kind of voice, "GOOD NIIIGHT, ELLIEEE!"

Ellie giggled, trying to think up another accent she could try. "I say, jolly good night, Bryony," she said, in as plummy an

English accent as she could muster up. She was pleased to hear Bryony's laugh.

"That sounded like my gran," Bryony said.

"Go on, your turn, Bryony," Grace called out.

"Okay," Bryony replied. "Let me think of one. Um . . . *Gooood niiiight, Elliee* . . ." she said in a spooky kind of whisper.

"Good night, Molleee!" Grace said in a little-girl voice.

"Nightie-night, Gra-a-ace!" Molly sang in a falsetto. "And nightie-night, Bryo-nee!"

There was a silence while everyone waited for Bryony to reply. Ellie found that she was holding her breath. *Come on, Bryony,* she thought. *Don't do this! Don't ignore Molly! She's done nothing wrong!*

After a few seconds, though, Bryony still hadn't replied. She *was* ignoring Molly!

"Bryony must have fallen asleep, Moll," Ellie said quickly, hoping to save Molly's feelings.

"Yeah," Molly replied, sounding doubtful. "Night, Ellie. Night, Grace. See you tomorrow."

Ellie lay in the darkness, thinking about what had happened. Molly would have to be kidding herself to believe that Bryony really had fallen asleep. Ellie was beginning to feel a little annoyed with Bryony. Sure, she was upset about missing Sophie—but they all were! And Molly being here didn't have anything to do with Sophie *not* being here. It wasn't as if Molly had pushed Sophie out herself.

Ellie could tell that none of the others were asleep yet, either. Nobody's breathing had deepened into the slow, regular breathing of sleep. Ellie shut her eyes quickly and willed herself to stop worrying. Bryony would get used to Molly being around soon. She just had to!

•   •   •   •

On Thursday, Ellie and the rest of the Year 8s had their first Irish dancing class.

Ellie was really looking forward to learning Irish dancing—and having their first mixed class with the boys. She'd seen Irish dancing performed on television a few times and loved watching it.

Their teacher was already waiting for them in the studio when they arrived. "Good afternoon, everyone," she said with a smile. "I'm Ms. Granger, and I hope you've still got some energy left for me this afternoon!"

"Just about," Matt joked, making the teacher smile.

"Glad to hear it," she said. "Because you'll need every ounce of energy for Irish dancing, believe me!"

"She's right, you know," Lara said, and then blushed as everyone looked at her—including their teacher.

"Am I right in thinking we have an Irish dancer already in the studio?" Ms. Granger asked with a smile.

Lara nodded. "Yes, Ms. Granger," she replied. "I've done a lot of it back in Ireland. I really love it!"

Ms. Granger looked pleased. "Excellent!" she said. "Let's hope the rest of you will like it as much. Now, sometimes we will be dancing in special clogs. But for most of the classes, you'll just wear your usual ballet shoes, which will help you get used to the steps. So . . . if you could all get into boy-girl partners, please? It might be easiest at first if you partner up with whomever you used to dance with in character class."

Ellie smiled as she and Matt made a beeline for each other. She was glad to be dancing with Matt again. He had been her regular partner for character dancing right through Year 7, and they knew each other's style very well.

When everybody was in pairs, Ms. Granger went on. "I'm going to be easy on you today, as it's your first week back," she said. "And I know it's hard to learn lots of new things when your bodies are still getting used to the shock of regular dancing again. We'll just start some preparatory work for a double jig rather than launching straight into it. I'll demonstrate a few steps for you to learn, and then you can have a turn."

The pianist began to play a jaunty tune, and Ellie watched with interest as her teacher clasped her hands in front of herself and began tapping out steps in time to the music. Her heeled character shoes clacked on the studio floor in a dizzying rhythm.

The students all burst into applause when Ms. Granger finished. "That looked *hard*," Ellie whispered to Matt.

He nudged her. "No worries, Ell—the dream team, that's us!—we'll have it sussed in no time."

Ms. Granger then showed them the steps more slowly so that everybody could get a better idea of how the dance was made up.

Then she asked each pair to link arms and walk through the first set of steps.

All was going well—until Ms. Granger decided that Luke and his partner, Megan, were a little cramped where they were dancing in one corner of the studio, and needed more room. "There's space over here, look," she said, pointing to a space next to Matt and Ellie. "Could you move over, please?"

It was quite ridiculous, Ellie knew, but as Luke loped over the studio toward her, she felt as if she had become rooted on the spot. Her face was split into a grin—a *moronic* kind of grin, as if she only had two brain cells!—and she couldn't drag her eyes away from Luke. He caught her looking over at him and grinned back, which promptly turned her face into a tomato all over again!

"Are you okay?" Matt asked as the music started up once more.

Ellie spun around guiltily to see that everyone else in the studio was walking through the steps again. Everyone except she and Matt, that is.

"You look a bit hot," Matt went on, his eyes concerned. "Do you want a drink of water or something?"

"No, no, I'm fine," Ellie said quickly. She grabbed his arm, trying to remember the steps they were supposed to be doing. Somehow Ms. Granger's instructions had floated clean out of her head.

"Ellie . . ." came Matt's uncertain voice. "Are you sure you're okay?"

"Fine," Ellie said, treading on his foot. "Just . . . getting used to it, that's all."

"And heel and toe . . . and finish," Ms. Granger's crisp voice said. "Some of you seemed to be struggling a little," she said, looking straight at Ellie. "Shall I run through it again?"

"Yes, please . . ." Ellie mumbled, feeling like an idiot. What must Luke think? She'd completely gone to pieces, and all because he was standing a few meters away from her! *Get a grip, Ellie Brown,* she told herself silently, *otherwise, it'll be really obvious to the whole WORLD that you've got a huge crush on Luke Bailey!*

Dear Diary,

The first Irish dancing class was sheer torture today. Not because I didn't like the dancing—I did! But because, with Luke nearby, I just couldn't do it properly to save my life. Goodness knows how many times I trod on Matt's toes and kicked him—and all because I was dancing near Luke. I mean, how tragic is that? How tragic am I???

I just hope I wasn't too obvious. I tried to laugh it off with Matt afterward, saying I just didn't have the luck of the Irish, or some other such feeble excuse—and he gave me this weird kind of look, like he thought I'd gone nuts. Oh, help! What's happening to me?

A bright autumn sun was shining through the windows of the ballet studio as Saturday's morning ballet class came to an end.

"*Now* it's the weekend!" Ellie said to Molly with a grin as they put their sweat suits back on. "Time for a whole day and a half of freedom!"

"What happens at weekends here?" Molly asked curiously. "I've been meaning to ask someone all week, but there have been so many other questions I've had in the meantime, I never got around to mentioning it."

"Well, I usually go home," Grace said, shaking her hair free from her bun as they walked up to the dorm to get showered. "To see my lovely dog—and my mum, too, of course! They'll be here to pick me up in half an hour or so."

"And Bryony often goes to her gran's for the weekend," Ellie told Molly. "She'll be off later this morning, too. Oh, and Holly and Alice go home quite often, as well. They don't live too far away, either. But the rest of us stay here most weekends. We sometimes go shopping in Sheen—I think there's a trip planned there this afternoon, if you want to go. Or sometimes there are day trips to

Richmond, or the West End. It changes every week."

"Isabelle, Kate, and I are going to Sheen later, if you want to join us," Lara put in, overhearing the conversation. "I know already what I'm going to order in our favorite café: black currant cheesecake and a cherry-choc shake!"

Ellie smiled. "Sounds good to me. What do you think, Moll? An afternoon of shopping, shakes, and cakes?"

"Count me in!" Molly said at once. "Now that you've mentioned the 'cake' word, it's a date!"

•   •   •   •

After Grace and Bryony had said their good-byes, Ellie and Molly both settled down to an hour of prep. "Hopefully, if we get a bit done now," Ellie reasoned, "we can have a completely guilt-free afternoon out without thinking about how much work we've got waiting for us."

"I'm going to start my 'Disaster Strikes!' essay," Molly decided. "I was thinking of setting it backstage at The Royal Ballet. Disaster strikes! The prima ballerina twists her ankle two minutes before she's due to dance in *Swan Lake*. Phew—what a relief—understudy Molly Baker steps up to take on the role." She grinned at Ellie. "And they all live happily ever after . . ."

Ellie laughed. "Like it. From disaster to dream come true," she said. "I'm going to write up my chemistry notes, I think. I'll have to keep thinking about the toffee crunch cake I'm going to have in Sheen—that's the only thing that will drive me on to finish!"

After an hour or so of quiet working, Ellie glanced up at the clock and realized it was almost time to catch the school minibus into Sheen. "Great—prep time is officially over, Moll!" she said, jumping up and grabbing her denim jacket and purse. "Let's go!"

Lara, Isabelle, and Kate were already on the minibus when Ellie and Molly went downstairs. The only spare seats were a pair directly across from Luke and Matt.

Ellie felt herself blush as they sat down. "Hi, guys," she said. She was trying to sound laid-back, but her voice seemed strangely loud and wobbly.

Luke was wearing a really nice pale blue T-shirt. Ellie noticed that it looked really good with his eyes. And his jeans were a trendy dark denim. Plus, he had really cool trainers . . .

"Ellie? Hey! Are you listening to me?"

As Molly's voice broke into her reverie, Ellie jumped guiltily. She quickly turned back. "Sure I am!" she replied. "Um . . . wait, what did you say again?" she asked, blushing an even deeper red. She was acting like such a ditz!

"You're miles away," Molly said good-naturedly. "Dreaming about your cake again, were you?"

"Something like that," Ellie said, glad that her new friend wasn't a mind reader.

Once they'd arrived in Sheen, the girls set off around the high street shops. Isabelle needed some new hairspray, and Lara wanted some emery boards, so they went to a drugstore first. Next, they went to a newsagent for magazines and candies.

While they were in there, Molly browsed through a rack of

postcards. "I need to send some to my friends," she said, picking out ones of the Queen of England, Buckingham Palace, and Big Ben. She laughed a little self-consciously. "Now, I know we're not exactly *in* the center of London, but as far as my friends back home are concerned, we may as well be. Do you think I'll get away with telling them I've been over to the Palace for afternoon tea with Prince William?"

Ellie giggled and pulled out a card that had a flying pig as an illustration. "You're more likely to see this than the Royal Family, but hey . . . don't let a little thing like the truth spoil your postcards," she told Molly.

After they'd bought everything they needed, the girls decided unanimously that it was time to revisit their favorite café. "We've spent many happy hours here," Ellie said to Molly as they went through its door.

"And consumed vast amounts of calories in the process," Kate added with a grin. "Thank goodness we burn them off so quickly!"

"Look—Matt, Luke, and Danny are here already," said Isabelle, pointing out the boys in the far corner, who were enthusiastically studying the menu.

Ellie glanced over to see Matt waving and beckoning them to join the guys. Oh, no! She couldn't decide if she wanted to sit with Luke or not. In an ideal world, she could think of nothing she'd like better than to be with him, talking and joking—but only if she could guarantee that she wouldn't turn bright red, she wouldn't laugh really loudly, and she would manage to get out at least one sentence that made sense! "Um . . . I'm not sure there's enough room for all of us," she said, feeling her cheeks grow hot.

But Matt was already on his feet, grabbing some extra chairs. "Of course there is," he said.

"Thanks, Matt," Kate said, sitting down and picking up a menu. "Ooh! New things on the menu!" she said as she started scanning through it. "Even better."

Ellie sat down and buried her nose in the menu. The others were all chatting a mile a minute, but she couldn't think of a single thing to say. Not one!

Everyone ordered their drinks first, deciding to take extra time to mull over the cake and dessert selection. It was never an easy decision when everything was so tempting—and with new choices on the menu, too . . . it was going to take them ages to decide.

"This is soooo good," Kate sighed, sipping her cherry-choc shake when it arrived. "I just love this café!"

"They even make good coffee," Isabelle agreed. "I do miss coffee at school!"

Luke had ordered coffee, too. "I'm with you there," he said, leaning across the table toward Isabelle. "Have you tried the cappuccinos here? Gorgeous!"

Ellie sipped her strawberry shake, wondering if it seemed a bit of a babyish drink to Luke. *Drinking coffee seems far more sophisticated,* she thought glumly. Maybe she should order one next time, even though she didn't really like the bitter taste.

"What cakes are people going to have, then?" Molly asked. "I think I've just about decided on a . . . strawberry shortcake."

"Good choice," Matt said approvingly. "Tried it many times—never been disappointed."

Isabelle fanned herself with the menu. "It is hot in here, no? Something cool would be perfect now. I think I shall go for a lemon sorbet."

"What was it you were going to have, Ellie? Toffee crunch cake?" Molly asked her.

Ellie bit her lip. "I'm not sure now," she said. She was having trouble enough *speaking* in front of Luke—how was she ever going to eat a piece of crumbly, crunchy cake in front of him? She would probably spray crumbs all over him—or drop loads of it down her shirt . . . and how attractive would that be? Not at all!

Maybe she should go for a sorbet, like Isabelle. Or maybe she should go something really grown-up? "I'll have a tiramisu, I think," she said, pronouncing it carefully. That was coffee-flavored, wasn't it? Maybe that would get Luke's approval.

She dared to glance over at him, and he was smiling at her. "A girl after my own heart, Ellie," he said. "Tiramisu is one of my favorites, too!" He scrutinized the menu again. "I'd just decided to have a banana split, but now I'm not so sure. Maybe I'll have to copy you with the tiramisu . . ."

"You can have a spoonful of mine, Luke, if you're still sold on the banana split," Ellie said, managing to smile at him even though her heart was pounding at his comment. Had he really just said that? *A girl after my own heart?* What was that supposed to mean? Had he guessed that she liked him? Was he saying that he liked her?

No, idiot, he was saying he likes tiramisu, she told herself firmly. *Now act normal, for goodness' sake!*

"Thanks," Luke replied. "Banana split it is, then—and I'll hold you to that spoonful of tiramisu, Ellie!"

The desserts arrived, and Ellie picked up her spoon rather hesitantly. If the truth were told, she'd never actually tried tiramisu. It looked nice, anyway: caramel colored, with chocolate sprinkles dotting the top of it. She dug in her spoon and tried some—then tried not to pull a face. Ugh! Coffee-tastic! How could anybody *like* that flavor?

"That looks good," Luke commented. He looked down at his banana split. "I wish I'd ordered tiramisu as well now," he added.

Ellie pushed her plate across to him. "Help yourself," she said. *And have as much as you want . . .* she added in her head. Then she wouldn't have to eat so much of it herself!

Lara laughed. "Wow—there's a first," she said. "Ellie Brown, sharing her dessert? What's got into you?"

Ellie blushed. Oh, no! She'd only offered it in the hope that Luke having some would mean she'd have less to eat herself. She didn't mean it to sound as if she was flirting with him! "Just . . . um . . . being kind," she said lightly. "How can I keep it all to myself when Luke is sitting there staring at it so longingly?"

Luke grinned. "Exactly what I was hoping," he said, taking his teaspoon from his coffee cup and helping himself to the tiramisu. "Mmmm! That is sooo good. Thanks, Ellie!"

"You're welcome," Ellie said, taking another mouthful herself. Ugh! Vile! *This is what you get for trying to impress Luke,* she told herself sternly. *It's all your own fault, Ellie Brown!*

•   •   •   •

After lights-out that evening, Ellie and Molly chatted for ages about all sorts of things. It was kind of nice, just the two of them.

"By the way, I hope you don't mind me asking," Molly said, when there was a pause in the conversation, "but is there something happening between you and Luke?"

"What?" Ellie gasped. She was glad the lights were out so Molly couldn't see the blush sweeping across her face. She seemed to be blushing all the time lately! "Why do you ask that?" she said.

"Well, you both seem to like each other," Molly pointed out, "and I couldn't help noticing that you've been going all twitchy around him—turning bright red and . . . "

"Oh, no," Ellie said quickly. "No, nothing's happening. You must have misunderstood. So . . . um . . ." she went on, frantically thinking of a way to change the subject, "tell me about Coventry."

Ellie found that she couldn't really concentrate as Molly began speaking about her home city. If Molly had guessed she liked Luke, did that mean the others had guessed, too? Did everyone know that she had a great big crush on him??

Ellie squeezed her eyes shut. Oh, she hoped not! She would just die if everyone knew that!

After a while, the conversation came back to school, and to the girls in their year.

"Ellie—I really need to know this," Molly said, her voice suddenly turning urgent. "Do you think Bryony is acting weird with me?"

Ellie hesitated. Boy—Molly was really coming out with the hard-hitting questions! "Well . . ." she began slowly, "Bryony's usually great—a really sweet person." She paused, trying to think of the right words to say. "But I know she's really upset about Sophie not being here . . ."

"I kind of guessed that," Molly put in dryly.

"And I know it's not an excuse, but I think that's why she's being a little cool with you," Ellie said.

"Because she thinks I'm trying to take Sophie's place," Molly concluded.

"Something like that," Ellie agreed. "But don't worry," she added quickly. "I'm sure Bryony will come around. You haven't done anything wrong. She would probably treat whoever the new person was the same."

"Right," Molly said.

But she didn't really sound reassured. Ellie couldn't blame her. She knew that she wouldn't have liked to be on the receiving end of Bryony's frostiness herself. She just hoped Bryony would snap out of it soon!

•　　　•　　　•　　　•

The second week of term began. Ellie was astonished to find that, before very long, the new schedule was starting to feel familiar. Ms. Swaisland's English classes were still proving to be really fun and inspiring—and Mr. Lewis's physics classes were hard to stay awake through!

On Thursday, it was their second Irish dancing class. Ellie was determined that she wouldn't get flustered if she had to dance anywhere near Luke this time, and warmed up well away from him, with quiet concentration. But then, almost as soon as she'd come into the room, Ms. Granger dropped a bombshell.

"Good afternoon, class," she greeted them. "This week, I'd like you to broaden your experience of dancing partners. So, rather than dancing with your usual partner, I'm going to swap you around."

A surprised gasp went around the room. Ms. O'Connor, their character teacher last year, had been quite happy for them all to stay with their regular partners each class. Ellie looked at Matt in shock. He was the only boy she'd ever danced with—even during the end-of-year performances last summer, they'd been partners.

"How shall we do this, I wonder?" Ms. Granger said. "Perhaps the simplest way would be if you all stand where you were last week. Boys, you all stay put. And girls—you all move along to the next boy on your right."

"So long, partner," Matt said, giving Ellie's arm a squeeze.

Ellie gave him a weak smile and, heart thumping, looked

over to her right, already knowing whom she would see standing there.

Luke.

Keep calm, Ellie, she instructed herself as she walked over to him. *Don't make it obvious how you feel, whatever you do!* But her trembling knees didn't seem to be listening.

"Hi, Luke," she managed to say in a faint voice.

"Hi, Ellie," he said, with one of his disarming smiles.

"Right, then!" said Ms. Granger, once everyone had been paired up. "We'll repeat the dance we learned last week. That way, you will know the steps and be able appreciate how it feels with a different partner."

She looked over at the pianist. "If you're ready, Mrs. Drake?"

The pianist began to play.

Luke put an arm around Ellie's waist and took her by the hand. "Ready?" he asked.

Ellie nodded, feeling unable to speak now. Luke Bailey actually had his arm around her! Luke Bailey was holding her hand!

"And . . . hop, gallop one, two, three . . ." Ms. Granger called. "On you go!"

Please don't let my hand get too sweaty where Luke's holding it, Ellie thought desperately. "Oops," she said as she stepped on Luke's foot. "Sorry, Luke." *Concentrate, Ellie! You're supposed to be dancing with him, not crippling him!*

"No worries," he said easily as they set off again.

Ellie felt as if she had two left feet—no, *three* left feet! If she wasn't treading on Luke, she was stumbling, or turning the wrong way. She'd fallen apart. She was hopeless!

"Are you okay, Ellie?" Luke asked after a moment. His eyes were concerned and quizzical.

Ellie took a deep breath and smiled. "I'm just not used to dancing with someone new, I guess," she said. "Sorry—I'm not usually this awful!"

"It *is* weird dancing with a new partner," Luke agreed, guiding her around as they as they continued the jig. "I guess we just have to get used to each other."

"I guess so," Ellie agreed, smiling up at him. She felt herself relax a little. They were only *dancing* together, after all.

As her body tuned into the rhythm of the music, Ellie felt her movements become more fluid again. And soon they were moving effortlessly around the studio.

"This is more like it," Luke said with a grin.

"It sure is," Ellie replied breathlessly. She knew they were dancing really well together now—she could feel it. It was as if their bodies were completely in sync moving as one together.

Too soon, the dance came to an end.

"That was great," Luke said, smiling down at her. "Once we got going, it was like we'd been partners forever!"

Ellie nodded, gazing back up into his gorgeous blue eyes. Her heart was thumping—and not just from the dancing. "It was, wasn't it?" she managed to mumble. "I enjoyed it, too." *And that,* she thought, trying not to giggle hysterically, *must be the understatement of the whole year!*

"I hope you all found working with a new partner a worthwhile exercise," Ms. Granger said with a smile, after the students had finished their reverence. "See you all next week."

The students all began to make their way out of the studio and collect their things from the corridor outside. Ellie felt as light as air—she had so enjoyed that class, she hadn't wanted it to end! It had been heavenly dancing with Luke—and she knew that he'd enjoyed it as well. *It was like we'd been partners forever,* he'd said. *What a nice thing to say . . .* she thought dreamily as she drank thirstily from her water bottle.

"Come on, Ellie—hurry up!" came Grace's voice. "I'm starving."

Ellie looked around to see her friend all ready to leave, whereas she hadn't even started putting on her sweat suit yet. "Sorry, Grace. Go ahead without me," she said. "I'll catch up with you." She hummed to herself as she pulled on her sweatpants. Luke was *such* a good dancer. And they had felt so *right* together. It was like there was just some chemistry between them.

Just then, Ellie's character teacher, Ms. O'Connor, came by. She said hello to Ellie as she passed, on her way into the studio. Looking around, Ellie realized that she was the only student left in the corridor. *My head is well and truly in the clouds these days,* she thought with a little smile. *I never even noticed!*

She heard Ms. Granger and Ms. O'Connor greet each other warmly.

"Good class?" Ellie then heard Ms. O'Connor ask.

"Great, thanks," Ms. Granger replied. "I got everyone to try dancing with a new partner. Some students seemed a little thrown by it at first—but most seemed to enjoy the experience."

Well, I sure did! Ellie thought with a smile. She picked up her water bottle and pushed it into her bag. As she turned to leave, Ms. Granger's next words floated over to her.

"Next week, I'll let them choose their own partners," she said. "That should prove interesting!"

Ellie froze in shock. Ms. Granger was planning to let *them* choose their partners next week? *No,* she thought. What if she had to choose between Matt—her lovely friend and usual dancing partner—and Luke, who made her feel like a prima ballerina?

Dear Diary,

    I can't stop thinking about what I overheard Ms. Granger say about next week's Irish dancing class! What am I going to do?

    I just don't know how I would choose between Matt and Luke, if I had to. I mean, I loved dancing with Luke today—it felt wonderful! But I'm almost sure that when Ms. Granger tells us we can dance with anybody we like, Matt will want us to go back to dancing together again. And if Luke did ask me to be his partner, I couldn't just drop Matt like a hot potato, could I? It would really hurt his feelings!

I haven't told anybody what I heard Ms. Granger say—I just want to keep it to myself until I've worked out what I'm going to do. And, of course, nobody really knows how I feel about Luke, so I don't even get to say any of this stuff out loud—it's all just going around and around in my head. Oh, everything is so complicated! I wish a fairy godmother would appear and figure all of this out for me!

Chapter 5

"And again, Molly . . . sharp *retiré*—whip that head, spot!"

It was the following Monday afternoon, and Ms. Black had singled Molly out again in their ballet class—this time, while they were practicing *pirouettes*. Molly's face was a little flushed as she obediently spun around through the movement alone.

"Prepare in fourth, Molly," Ms. Black said, coming to reposition Molly's back foot a fraction. "Try to keep your fingers together this time—like this, see?"

Molly looked a little ashamed as she watched Ms. Black demonstrate again for her. Ellie felt a pang of sympathy. Now that they were in the third week of term, Ms. Black seemed to have stepped their class up a notch. They were back on pointe, they were learning new routines—and Ms. Black seemed to be singling Molly out for just about everything today. Their grace period was up: Now the work had started in earnest.

At the end of class, Ellie's body ached, but her heart was singing. She was starting to feel like she was back on form now—she was leaping higher, stretching farther, and dancing far better than she had at the beginning of term.

But Molly didn't look so happy. In fact, she looked downright miserable, Ellie thought as they put on their sweat suits after class.

"Are you all right, Molly?" Ellie asked softly as they left the studio.

Molly sighed. "Oh, Ellie . . . don't get me wrong—I love ballet, and I am still thrilled to be here at The Royal Ballet School, but . . ." She shrugged, a doleful expression spreading over her face. "Sometimes I think Ms. Black doesn't like me at all! She picks on me all the time—for everything I do!"

"She's just trying to help you, Molly," Ellie replied in surprise. "It's not about not liking you."

"But I feel such a failure," Molly said. "I can't do anything— not even barre exercises—without her coming over to correct me, or tell me what I'm doing wrong." She heaved a heavy sigh as they turned into the corridor that led to the Billiard Room. "I don't know. Maybe I'm not cut out for The Royal Ballet School after all."

"Oh, Molly, don't say that!" protested Grace, joining in the conversation. "Ms. Black only corrects you because she thinks you're worth the trouble," she reasoned. "If she didn't think so, she wouldn't be putting in all the extra coaching. She wants you to stay—she wants you to be good enough."

"And don't forget," Ellie added, "the rest of us have already had a whole year to get used to The Royal Ballet School's technique—some of us even longer, if we were JAs before starting

Lower School. You just need time to catch up."

"I guess so," Molly said, sounding a little brighter. "It's just hard to carry on when you keep getting criticized, that's all."

"I can imagine," Ellie said sympathetically. "But you ask any of us—or any of the older students—and they'll tell you that getting attention from the teachers is a good thing, even if it might not seem that way right now." But privately, Ellie was becoming a little worried for Molly. She really was getting critiqued, it seemed, on almost every detail of her ballet technique.

Molly smiled, but the smile didn't quite reach her eyes.

"You'll be *fine*," Ellie said in a firm voice as they went into the dorm. "Ms. Black just wants you to be even better."

"What's up?" Bryony asked. She was already in the dorm, having gone ahead at the end of the lesson.

"Molly's afraid that that Ms. Black thinks she can't cut it here," Ellie said. "But we all know she can, right?"

Bryony shrugged. "It's up to Ms. Black, not us," she said dismissively, and then she headed off toward the bathroom.

"Oh, great," Molly said, throwing her water bottle down on her bed. "So Bryony doesn't think I'm good enough to be a student here, either!"

"I'm sure she didn't mean it that way!" Ellie said at once, going to put an arm around Molly. But she caught the shocked look on Grace's face as she did so—and guessed that Grace had interpreted Bryony's remark the same way. By not being supportive of Molly, Bryony had just made the new girl feel even worse—and Ellie was sure that Bryony had done so deliberately.

•   •   •   •

The following day, Ellie stood in the lunch queue, worrying about the Irish dancing class in two days' time. It had been on her mind since she'd overheard Ms. Granger's conversation. She hated the thought of potentially having to choose between Matt or Luke. Maybe, she thought suddenly, if Ms Granger did announce they were to choose their own partners in Thursday's class, Ellie could pretend she hadn't really been paying attention. That way, when everyone rushed around, choosing whomever they wanted, she could stand there, pretending to be confused. *What? What are we doing?* she imagined herself saying. And, then, hopefully, somebody would just choose her, and she wouldn't have to choose someone over someone else. Or maybe . . .

"Ellie, if you stare at that pasta tray any harder, it'll probably start confessing all its innermost secrets to you!"

Ellie almost jumped out of her skin at the sound of Luke's voice. She hadn't even noticed she was standing right in front of the pasta dishes, let alone that she seemed to be staring at them. "Oh, er . . . hi, Luke," she said, trying not to look flustered. "Just trying to make up my mind . . ." *And not about the pasta,* she told herself wryly.

Luke started chatting away to her, but all Ellie could think about was the next Irish dancing class, and what might happen. Was there really a chance he'd ask her to be his partner?

"So, anyway, I'll see you later," Luke suddenly said, taking a plate of Spaghetti Bolognese. "Hope you make your mind up soon!"

Ellie blinked. *Oh, my goodness!* She hadn't listened to a word he'd said to her. She must have been standing there the whole time, looking vacant and not saying a thing back. What must he have thought?

She picked up some Spaghetti Bolognese, too—and then changed her mind. He'd think she was copying her if she chose that now. She put back the spaghetti and picked up a plate of cannelloni instead. But, actually, she really did prefer the look of the spaghetti . . .

"Come on, love—they're *both* delicious!" the woman behind the pasta counter said in amusement. "You're creating a traffic jam!"

Ellie grabbed the spaghetti and walked away quickly, her cheeks flaming. She wished she could just start this lunchtime all over again!

•　　　•　　　•　　　•

That evening, Ellie and the rest of the Year 8 girls hung out in the Billiard Room in their pajamas. Talk soon turned to the boys.

"Oliver Stafford thinks he's sooo gorgeous, doesn't he?" said Lara.

Alice groaned out loud. "Tell me about it! I still haven't recovered from dancing with him in Irish dancing class last week," she said. "I hope I don't have to partner him on Thursday, too. There's no way I want to dance with him again—but someone will have to!"

" 'Disaster Strikes!' " Megan and Holly said at the same time, and then fell about, giggling.

"Well, *I'm* not having him back," Scarlett retorted. She had been Oliver's regular partner in character class last year. "I hope Ms. Granger says we have to stick with our *new* partners. I much preferred dancing with Toby last Thursday."

Molly looked mystified. "What's so awful about dancing with Oliver?" she asked.

"Where shall I begin?" Scarlett replied darkly. "For starters, he thinks he's the greatest dancer on the planet, and that it's a real honor for you to dance with him!"

"He made me feel like that, too," Alice grumbled. "Like he was doing me some kind of favor by being his partner for the class!"

"Oliver *is* quite good-looking, though," Molly countered.

"Looks aren't everything," Scarlett replied. "He's arrogant and bossy with it. Plus, he has the hottest hands you've ever felt!"

"That bad, huh?" Molly asked with a grin.

"WORSE!" the girls chorused, with feeling—Ellie included, this time. She'd never had to partner him for a whole class, but during many of the routines they'd danced in character class last year, girls and boys had had to swap partners within the dance. Oliver's hot sweaty hands had become something of a legend!

Molly giggled. "I'm kind of intrigued about Oliver, now," she said. "I like a challenge—maybe I'll try to partner him on

Thursday."

"Yes! Please!" the others chorused, laughing.

•   •   •   •

The next morning at breakfast, there were a few knowing glances between the Year 8 girls as Oliver approached the table and sat down at the far end.

"There's your man, Moll," Megan whispered, with a grin on her face.

"Stand by your ma-a-a-n," Ellie sang tunelessly.

"What's all this about?" Matt asked, getting wind of the conversation. "Molly—are you and Oliver an item?"

Ellie and the others hooted with laughter.

"No!" Molly spluttered, almost dropping her cornflakes spoon as she put up her hands in a *Whoa!* gesture. "No, I—"

" 'Disaster Strikes!' " said Scarlett, and everyone went into a fresh wave of giggles.

Quite a few other students had turned to see what all the Year 8 girls had found so amusing. Matt looked from one girl to another, too, trying to work out the joke.

"Sorry, Matt," Ellie said, realizing that her friend was feeling left out. "Ignore us. Private joke."

"You lot!" Molly hissed. "No more comments about me and you-know-who. That's how rumors get started."

"Sorry, Molls," Lara said. She bit off a corner of her toast. "Hey, it was fun last night, wasn't it, us all being in the Billiard Room together? It felt like old times, when we were Year 7s, all sharing that great big dorm."

Kate's face lit up. "Maybe we could all get together for a midnight feast one night?" she suggested in a low voice.

Everyone agreed it was a great idea.

"How about next Friday?" suggested Isabelle.

"Excellent," Ellie said happily. "It's a date!"

"Who's got a date?" Luke asked just then, coming over with his breakfast tray. His eyes fell upon Ellie. "What's this? Has somebody got a boyfriend I didn't know about?"

Ellie blushed. "No—nobody's going on any dates," Ellie said quickly, not wanting Luke to get the wrong idea. The last thing she wanted him to think was that she was dating somebody else!

Dear Diary,

It's our Irish dancing class tomorrow—and I still don't know whether to dread it or feel excited about it.

I'm kind of hoping that Matt just turns to me and assumes I'll be partnering him as usual. At least that takes all the stress out of the whole thing.

But, of course, I'm also secretly hoping that Luke wants to dance with me again . . .

I just can't help wishing for it!

Ellie was so preoccupied by the thought of the Irish dancing class at the end of the day that she could hardly concentrate during Thursday morning's lessons. And geography, biology, and physics were three of her absolute least-favorite subjects anyway!

Back in the dorm at the end of the morning, Ellie sat on her bed, shaking her head, surveying the pile of schoolbooks in front of her. She realized that she was clueless about how to do her physics prep, utterly baffled by the scribbled notes she'd made in geography—and as for biology, she'd spent ages diligently copying out all the parts of a flower from her textbook during the lesson only to discover that she'd been on the wrong page the whole time, and the rest of the class had copied out leaf structures. *Not your best academic performance, Ellie Brown,* she thought. She sighed, and then followed the others down to lunch.

•   •   •   •

Ellie managed to keep her focus throughout ballet class that afternoon—partly because Luke wasn't within the same four walls, and partly because she'd always found that throwing herself into ballet was a good way to work through any problems she had. Somehow or other, while she was engrossed in the technicalities of dancing, other things seemed to drift out of her mind temporarily.

Today, Ms. Black was focusing on their *changement battu.* "They need to be neater, and the beat crisper," she announced. "Really cross the feet, and pass through first in the air. So, when you're ready . . . off we go."

The music started, and the students set to work. Almost at once, Ms. Black was at Molly's side. Ellie saw Molly's shoulders slump in dejection.

Bryony, who was standing next to Ellie today, rolled her eyes. "Sophie had to leave because she was struggling in class, but Molly struggles even more! Why does she deserve to be here more than Sophie?" she whispered angrily.

Ellie shook her head. "I don't think you can compare them like that, Bry," she whispered back. "Molly's still finding her feet here—literally!"

But Bryony just rolled her eyes again.

Ellie sighed and turned back to her exercises. Ms. Black was still talking to Molly. "Try to keep your head still when you're jumping up," she was saying. "And remember to keep your upper half straight—relax your arms, try not to take the tension in your upper body."

After a while, Ms. Black asked them to try another step. "*Entrechat quatre* next," she said. "Again, neatly done, with crisp beats every time, please. The front foot has to change to the back in the air, and return to the front on landing," she instructed. "Everybody ready? And off we go . . ."

Ellie became so engrossed in the *entrechats* that, before she knew it, the class was almost over. And after cooling down with some stretches, it was time to have a well-earned snack from their tuck boxes before changing for their Irish dancing class.

Irish dancing class!

Otherwise known as crunch time . . .

•   •   •   •

This was it—the class Ellie had been thinking about all week. Her heart began to pound as she began her warm-up exercises. Would it be Matt? Or Luke?

"Hello, everyone," Ms. Granger said, coming into the studio. "Everybody warmed up? Good. Now, this week, I'd like you to choose your own partner. You can go back to your usual partner if you want, or hook up again with your new partner from last week—or some of you more adventurous souls might want to try *another* new partner!"

There was a buzz of excitement as students began pairing up. Off went Grace toward Danny, her regular partner . . . Off went Megan toward Justin . . . And there was Molly, with a cheeky grin, heading straight toward Oliver!

Ellie just stood there, frozen to the spot. *Oh, help!* she thought. *What should I do?*

Feeling flustered, she began to gaze around the crowded studio—and immediately caught sight of Luke. He was also still on his own. And he was looking straight at her! Did that mean . . . ?

Ellie smiled at him encouragingly. *Come here, Luke,* she silently urged him. *Come here and ask me!*

"You and me then, Ell?" called a voice to her right.

Ellie turned to see Matt strolling toward her, clearly assuming they would be partners again. She flicked her eyes helplessly back toward Luke.

Oh, no! He'd turned away now.

Ellie turned back to Matt, finding it impossible to disguise the disappointment flitting across her face.

Seeing all this, Matt's step faltered. Ellie registered the hurt puzzlement in his eyes and felt a stab of remorse. What was she thinking? She plastered a smile over her face and went toward her buddy.

Matt's expression cleared immediately, and Ellie knew she'd done the right thing. She slipped her arm through his and tried to ignore what she could see from the corner of her eye.

Alice walking over to Luke . . .

Luke smiling and nodding . . .

Luke linking arms with Alice . . .

Alice—Luke's new partner.

Ellie had done the right thing. She definitely had. So why did it feel so wrong?

Dear Diary,

The whole choosing partners thing in our Irish dancing class today was as awful as I'd dreaded it would be! It all happened in about five seconds—yet it seemed to go on for about five minutes. I keep replaying the scene over and over again—watching it in my head, like a movie:

At one end of the studio is Luke without a partner, looking at me . . .

But then there's Matt—my good buddy Matt—coming toward me and expecting things to stay as usual. How could I let him down? I just couldn't!

And there is Luke again, losing interest in me now that Matt has asked me, turning away . . .

. . . and turning to Alice instead.

Does she like him, too, I wonder? I bet she does—I mean, who wouldn't? He's so funny and good-looking and such a brilliant dancer . . . and now he's her partner, not mine.

And to make matters worse, Ms. Granger is going to think I'm such a terrible dancer! I keep going to pieces in her lessons. The problem is, all I can think about is Luke, and what would have happened if I'd just gone over to him from the start and asked if he wanted to be partners again.

He might have said no. But he also might have said yes. And now I'll never know.

Oh, I wish I could get the whole thing out of my head!

I can't even talk about it to anybody because I don't want anyone to know how I feel about Luke.

Aaaargghh!!

P.S. What if Luke starts liking Alice??

* * * *

The following evening, after Mrs. Parrish's footsteps had died away along the corridor, following nine o'clock lights-out, Ellie lay in her bed, her heart thudding with excitement. Tonight was the night of the midnight feast! She and the rest of the Year 8 girls had all agreed earlier to stay quiet in bed for half an hour, so that Mrs. Parrish would be fooled into thinking they'd settled down to sleep. Then the fun would start, with everybody invited around to the west side of the Billiard Room for the feast!

The half an hour seemed to take ages to pass! But eventually, there was a soft knocking at the door of the Room Off, and Ellie, Grace, Molly, and Bryony all dived out of their beds.

Ellie had managed to smuggle a *pain au chocolat* up to the dorm after breakfast (and had a pocket full of flaky pastry to prove it), plus she'd managed to sneak out her gummy bears and an apple from her tuck box, too.

Grace, meanwhile, was retrieving half a packet of chocolate biscuits and a bag of raisins from where she'd stashed them under her bed. Molly was unearthing a slab of chocolate from her wardrobe and two bags of potato chips from her shoe bag, and Bryony had a bag of crackers and some grapes that she'd just taken out of her underwear drawer!

"Everyone ready?" Ellie hissed, shining her flashlight around the room.

"Yes," the others whispered together.

"Let's go, then!" Ellie said, opening the door as quietly as she could. She led the way into the Billiard Room, where she could already see flashlights bobbing about through the darkness. Most of the other girls had already gathered in the west end of the room, with a great assortment of food and drink between them.

The last two girls, Holly and Rebecca, made their way over from the other end of the dorm—Holly juggling some juice cartons up in the air. "We come bearing gifts!" she giggled. "Oops! Sorry, Megan, did that one get you?" she said as one of the cartons went wildly astray.

Megan rubbed the top of her head, but she was smiling. "It's lucky you're training to be a ballerina, not a circus clown," she told Holly, and then turned to the others. "Right—who wants a *croissant*, then?" she added, producing two from her dressing gown pocket with a flourish. "They're a bit squashed, but still yummy," she announced, biting the end off one of them.

There was a rustling and ripping open of bags and wrappers as the goodies were shared around. The girls all made themselves comfortable, perched on the west end beds, or on pillows on the floor.

"Does anyone know any good games?" Molly asked after they'd been eating and drinking for a while. "Hey—how about Truth or Dare?" she suggested brightly. "I'm sure everyone knows that one."

"Oh, not Truth or Dare—that's so Year 7," Bryony said rather scornfully.

Molly looked a little taken aback. "What, you mean you think it's babyish?" she asked.

"We've played it so many times, it's a bit boring," Bryony said, not meeting Molly in the eye. "Besides, I know everything I want to know about everyone here already."

"Well, you don't know any of *my* secrets," Molly countered.

Bryony raised her eyebrows rather sarcastically, but didn't comment.

Right, thought Ellie, *so basically you're saying you don't want to know any of Molly's secrets! How rude, Bryony!*

There was an awkward silence. Ellie hated the way Bryony had left Molly's comment hanging in the air so dismissively. "How about telling *us* one of your secrets then, Moll," she suggested quickly. "Or . . . wait, I know. Give us five facts about yourself— one true, the others lies. And we have to guess which is which."

To Ellie's relief, Molly smiled. "Okay," she said. "Now, let me think." She chewed a bit of *croissant* for a couple of moments, and then smiled. "Right—I've got my facts. So only one of them is true, right?"

"Hit us with them!" Kate urged.

"Right, well, the first fact is that my middle name is . . . Ethel," Molly said.

Kate and Lara burst out laughing at that.

"Ethel?" Lara hooted.

"Don't laugh. That could be the true one!" Molly reminded them. "Fact number two . . ." she went on. "I am really terrified of sharks."

"Ooh, yes," Megan said teasingly. "Because we get so many of those in England, don't we? Not!"

"All right, all right!" Lara laughed. "Let Molly finish!"

"Fact number three—I am related to the Royal Family," Molly said, her face still poker-straight.

"No way!" Ellie cried, peering at her new friend's expression. That couldn't be true, could it?

"Fact number four—I once ate worms as a dare," Molly went on, her eyes sparkling. "And fact number five—after dancing with him yesterday, I'm now madly in *lurrve* with Oliver Stafford."

There were guffaws of laughter from everyone at the last fact.

"Pouf! Well, we all know that one cannot possibly be true," dismissed Isabelle.

"Not unless you had a lobotomy last night while we weren't watching," added Scarlett drily.

"I saw that fierce look you gave him when he trod on your toes," Megan laughed. "I thought he was going to keel over with shock!"

Molly grinned impishly, but said nothing.

"It has to be the worms," Kate declared.

"No—I say the sharks," Grace said, shaking her head at Kate.

"I don't think it is, but I really hope number three is true—that you're related to the Royal Family," Ellie declared with a grin.

"What was the first one? Oh, Ethel," Lara remembered. "Well, you don't look like an Ethel to me!"

"Unless her granny was an Ethel?" Megan suddenly suggested. "I mean, my middle name is Bertha, after my granny. Bertha! I ask you!"

"I'm bored with this now. Anybody fancy playing a game of cards?" Bryony said abruptly, producing a pack from her drawer.

Once again, there was an awkward pause and the jolly mood vanished.

"Well, we haven't finished Molly's truth game yet," said Lara rather pointedly.

"Obviously Bryony isn't the slightest bit interested," Molly said with a tight little laugh.

"*I* am, though," Ellie said quickly, wanting to avoid a scene. "And *I* think that the true fact is number—" But before she could finish, Molly interrupted.

"So tell me, Bryony," she went on. "Why *exactly* don't you want to have anything to do with me? You've been off with me ever since I arrived here."

With a sinking heart, Ellie saw that Molly's eyes were now glittering with anger. She had been pushed too far this time, and the anger was making her brave.

Bryony said nothing.

"Come on, Bryony," Molly insisted. "I'd really love to know. Why don't you just tell me what the problem is, so it's out in the open once and for all."

But Bryony remained silent.

"Is it because I'm not Sophie?" Molly asked. "Because if it is, that stinks! It's not my fault that Sophie was assessed out! And even if I hadn't joined this class, Sophie *still* wouldn't be here with you. She's gone. And now I'm here instead. And I can't stand you treating me like you think I'm inferior anymore!"

There was a shocked silence as Molly finished speaking. All eyes turned to Bryony, who promptly burst into tears and ran to the bathroom.

"I'll go after her," Ellie said, jumping up. She hurried over to the bathroom, feeling a little dazed. That had been some outburst from Molly. She must have been bottling that up for ages! Ellie felt for Bryony, being confronted like that. But on the other hand, she couldn't help feeling that Molly had been absolutely right to stand up for herself.

"Bryony?" Ellie said, knocking softly on the bathroom door.

"It's me, Ellie. Can I come in?" She heard Bryony blow her nose.

"It's not locked," came Bryony's muffled voice.

Ellie pushed open the door to see Bryony leaning against one of the sinks, tears still streaming down her cheeks. "Bryony—what has all this been about?" she asked. "*I've* noticed you being off with Molly, too—I think everyone has. Is she right about why you've been acting that way?"

Bryony wiped her eyes with a tissue. "Sort of . . ." she confessed. "But it's not just about Sophie . . ." she went on. "I just can't bear to see *anyone* replaced like that—like they're just so dispensable!"

Ellie put an arm around her. "But like Molly said," she went on gently, "she didn't have anything to do with Soph being assessed out. And what would *we* have done in Molly's shoes?" she added. "We'd have taken the spare place, too, wouldn't we?"

Bryony gave a miserable sniff and then nodded. "I know. You're right. And I know I've been horrible to Molly. But . . ." Her eyes filled with tears again.

"But what?" Ellie asked softly. Her friend looked so sad.

Bryony blew her nose again. "I feel like everything around me is changing, Ellie." She swallowed hard and then went on. "Last Easter my mum and dad told me they were going to get a divorce . . ."

Ellie gasped. "Oh, no! Why didn't you say anything about this before?"

"I just wanted to shut it all out while I was here at school,"

Bryony explained quietly. "And I really, really hoped that they'd change their minds. But then, over the summer holidays, Dad took me to his new apartment—and there was *Wendy* . . . she's living there with him." Bryony turned bewildered, tear-filled eyes to Ellie. "He's replaced Mum—just like that! How can you just substitute one person for another? It made me so hurt and angry, Ellie!"

"Have you told your dad how you feel?" Ellie asked.

Bryony shook her head. "I couldn't talk to him. I had this . . . it was like a tight *knot* of pain and anger in my chest the whole time I was there. I couldn't wait to leave and get back to Mum. And then, when I got back here—"

"Molly had taken Sophie's place," Ellie finished for her. "But Bryony"—Ellie struggled to find the right words—"of course you don't think there's anybody as good as your own mom. I feel the same about mine. And we both know that there's only one Sophie Crawford in the world. But that doesn't mean that Molly and your dad's girlfriend can't be great people, too."

There was pause. And then Bryony heaved a long, shaky sigh. "I haven't given either of them a chance," she admitted. "And I've punished Molly when she's done nothing wrong."

"And now Molly is hurting, too," Ellie said quietly.

Bryony nodded. She blew her nose one last time, and then balled up the tissue and threw it in the bin. "I know. And it's high time I went and said sorry," she said decisively.

Ellie hugged her friend. They left the bathroom and went back to the Billiard Room.

As they walked in, all eyes were on Bryony. She took a deep breath. "Molly, I owe you an apology," she said. "A big one. I haven't been very nice to you at all—and I'm really, really sorry. It's not your fault Sophie had to leave, and I shouldn't have taken my feelings out on you."

Ellie turned toward Molly, wondering how she was going to respond.

Molly nodded. "Thank you, Bryony," she said quietly. "And I'm sorry I shouted at you."

Bryony shrugged. "You were right to," she replied. "I'd have shouted at me, too!"

Molly gave Bryony a tentative smile. "Friends, then?" she asked.

Bryony smiled back and nodded. A tear rolled down her cheek, and she dashed it away with her dressing gown sleeve. "Friends," she agreed.

"Oh, don't cry—you'll set me off!" Molly exclaimed, her eyes now glistening with tears, too. "See? It always happens!" She grabbed a tissue out of her pocket and blew her nose really loudly.

"Whoa!" exclaimed Bryony. "That's even louder than my granddad!"

Everyone roared with laughter—and, with it, Ellie felt the tension in the dorm begin to disappear.

"Shh, shh!" said Grace, still giggling herself. "We don't want

Mrs. Parrish up here!"

"Well if my honking didn't wake her, nothing will!" Molly retorted.

The noise level rose a bit further as everyone cracked up again.

"Seriously, though, girls," Molly said, "you might not be laughing in the summer—I get hay fever! My nose-blowing drives my family mad!"

"So . . ." said Kate, "are we having this midnight feast, or what?"

"Good point," said Molly, taking a handful of potato chips and wedging them into her mouth.

"By the way, Molly," said Bryony, as she leaned over for a handful of potato chips herself, "what *was* the true fact?"

"Number one," Molly replied as she munched. "My middle name really is Ethel."

"No!" Ellie felt her eyes widen in shock. "Molly Ethel Baker? Really?"

Molly burst out laughing and shook her head. "Fortunately not," she chuckled. "I was just winding you up—my middle name is Anna!"

"So what was it, then? The Royal Family one?" Ellie guessed hopefully.

Molly shook her head. "Sorry, girls. Kate's the only one around here with famous parents."

"Please tell me it's not the being-in-lurvve-with-Oliver one?"

Lara asked, her eyes wide.

"No way," Molly said. "You were right, all of you—never again will I be so crazy as to voluntarily partner that boy. Mr. Stuck-up I'm-the-greatest-dancer—with the hottest hands in the universe!"

"I'm glad to hear it," Lara said.

"We did try to warn you," Alice laughed.

"You did," Molly agreed. "But as I told you, I can't resist a challenge—which is why my true fact was . . . that I ate worms. My brother dared me to eat some when I was five. They were gross, but I did it." She grinned. "And my mum went crazy, I can tell you!"

"Oh, yuck!" Grace squealed.

"I think you should have learned your lesson after the worms," Ellie said with a grin. "Just because someone dares you into something, you don't have to do it!"

Molly laughed. "You're right, there," she said cheerfully. "I didn't learn, did I?" She helped herself to another handful of potato chips. "Still, eating worms does make me appreciate good food now."

"Hear hear!" Kate said, waving a half-eaten candy bar in the air. "Here's to midnight feasts: good food—and good friends!"

"Good food and good friends," the others all chorused—even Bryony.

Dear Diary,

Just writing this very quickly by my flashlight before I go to sleep. I think the others have already dozed off. We're all ready to burst from all the food!

Everything came to a head with Molly and Bryony tonight. It was pretty intense, I can tell you. But it's such a relief to have everything out in the open: Bryony admitted why she's been so snotty to Molly and she apologized. And now that the air has cleared, things seem to be okay between them.

In fact, I have a feeling that now that Bryony is willing to give Molly a chance, they're going to get on really well. After all, Molly has got the same mad sense of humor that Bryony likes so much in Sophie.

So fingers crossed that everything will be happier in the dorm from here onward!

Chapter 7

The following week in Irish dancing class, Ms. Granger told everybody to stay with the partners they'd chosen last week.

She said the same thing the week after that, too!

Molly wasn't happy about this one bit, as it meant she was partnered with Oliver three weeks in a row. "I think I'd rather be eating worms," she said gloomily, after the third class.

Ellie wasn't happy about the arrangement, either. She tried to kid herself that she wasn't bothered, and that of course, she'd much rather be partners with Matt. But that second week, she kept finding her gaze drifting across to where Luke was swinging Alice around in the jig . . . and then every now and then she'd hear the sound of Alice giggling as the pair of them shared a joke about something or other. It made Ellie's heart pound with jealousy each time. That might have been her!

Ellie couldn't help but brood about the closeness that seemed to have sprung up between Luke and Alice. She found herself looking more closely at Alice whenever she got the chance. She really was very pretty, with her long, tawny-colored hair, clear skin, and green eyes. Luke surely thought she was pretty, didn't he? And Alice had such gorgeous clothes. She had great dress sense, and never wore anything scruffy or clashing. She was much "girlier" than Ellie would ever be. Her hair was always combed and shiny, and her nails were always neatly filed and buffed. Maybe Luke liked that about her, too.

•   •   •   •

"Alice, can you give me a hand with my math prep later on?" she heard Luke say as they sat down to lunch the next day. "I don't have a clue what Mr. Best was going on about this morning—and you seemed to be able to answer all of his questions, so . . ."

"Oh, flattery will get you everywhere, Luke Bailey," Alice replied with a grin. "Shall we get together after supper tonight?"

"Great," Luke said. "Look forward to it."

Look forward to it! The words were like a stab to Ellie's heart. If only she didn't stink at math. Then she could have put *her* hand up to answer more of Mr. Best's questions, and Luke might have turned to *her* for help instead!

•   •   •   •

The following Monday, Ellie heard Luke talking to Alice about a novel she'd lent him, as the students all gathered in the canteen for tuck.

"You were right, it's fantastic," he told her.

"Glad you're enjoying it," Alice replied with a smile.

"Um . . . what book's that?" Ellie asked, deliberately joining the conversation in the hope it was something she'd read, too.

"It's a horror kind of thing," Luke replied. "It's called

Evilheart."

Ellie's heart sank. She hadn't read it, not really liking that kind of book. "Is it about Dr. Warburton?" she joked. They'd had chemistry that morning, and Dr. Warburton had been in a particularly evil mood.

Luke laughed. "Different evil-heart," he said. "I think the book that you're thinking of is *Chemist of Doom.*"

"Or *Prep-setter from Hell,*" Ellie giggled, warming to her theme. "Or maybe—"

"I read somewhere they're making *Evilheart* into a film next year," Alice said, smiling her sweet smile again. "I bet it'll be an adults-only rating, though. It's sooo scary!"

Ellie shut her mouth with a snap. Why did Alice have to interrupt her like that? Luke had just been laughing with her, as well—and now the moment had gone.

Later that evening, Ellie and a whole group of other students— Grace, Lara, Molly, Bryony, Matt, Luke, and six or seven others— had been hanging out by the pool table downstairs, getting ready to pick teams for a mini-tournament, when Alice came by with Scarlett.

"Fancy a game of pool, you two?" Luke called out straightaway.

Alice's face lit up. "Sure!" she said.

Ellie really struggled not to feel too annoyed that Alice and Luke wound up on the same team while she ended up on a team with Grace, Matt, and Toby.

Luke was a brilliant pool player, and his team won comfortably. Ellie could hardly bear to watch as he celebrated with his teammates.

"Yes!" he cheered, hugging Alice, as the team all congratulated each other. "We are the champions!"

Worst of all, Ellie observed that evening as she was getting ready for bed, was the fact that Alice was a really nice person. She was funny and kind, with a great sense of humor. Ellie wished she could dislike her just a little bit! It was impossible, though. Everybody liked Alice.

●　　　●　　　●　　　●

Ellie was still brooding about it all as she got changed for her Friday afternoon ballet class later that week. She cringed as she remembered what had happened this morning at breakfast.

A sign had appeared on the Year 8 notice board about a forthcoming trip to see *The Lion King* in a West End theater after the half-term break.

"Are you going to put your name down for the *Lion King trip*, Ellie?" Luke asked her with a smile.

Ellie's heart started pounding as she looked across the table into his laughing blue eyes, willing herself not to do her tomato impression again. "Oh, yes, definitely," she told him. She hadn't really given much thought to going, but if Luke was planning to, that was a different story.

"Great," Luke said. "It's meant to be brilliant, isn't it?"

Ellie nodded, her heart rate moving up yet another gear as a thought struck her: *Is he kind of asking me on a date??*

"How about you, Matt?" Luke asked. "Are you up for the *Lion King* trip?"

Ellie slumped over her porridge bowl, her heart sinking in disappointment. *Stupid, Ellie!* she chastised herself. *He was just being friendly!*

As she left the canteen, Ellie decided it was time to pull herself together—to get over her silly crush on Luke. And she made a real effort not to look at him during the morning's lessons. But then, at lunchtime, he had come over and told her he liked the way she'd braided her hair—and her new resolve had disappeared! Surely Luke's noticing her hairstyle was a sign that he liked her a little bit?

Ellie sighed as she now undid the braids and began fixing her hair into a bun for ballet class. Maybe Luke was just one of those people who was friendly to everybody, she thought miserably. And, for all she knew, he might not have any *special* feelings for either her *or* Alice.

"Arghh! My hair is just all over the place today!" Molly cried, breaking into Ellie's thoughts.

"Do you want a hand?" Bryony offered at once.

"Please," Molly said gratefully. "My fingers keep getting tangled up with each other today, if you know what I mean."

"We all know that one," Grace said sympathetically.

"Let's have a look," Bryony said, going over to Molly with her hairbrush at the ready. "Whoa! How much hairspray have you got on here? It's like candy floss!"

"I know," Molly giggled. "Mind your fingers don't get glued together in there . . . I got a bit carried away, and . . ."

"You can say that again," Bryony said, but she was giggling too.

Ellie smiled to herself as Bryony and Molly joked around about Molly's sticky hair catching stray flies. It was so good to see those two becoming such friends, now that the air had been cleared between them. Bryony seemed to be doing everything she could to make Molly feel right at home now, here in Lower School.

"There," Bryony said, when she'd tamed Molly's hair into a neat bun.

"Brilliant, thanks," Molly said, checking her reflection. She twisted her mouth in a funny little smile. "Now, if you could just sort out my ballet for me, too, Bryony, my life would be completely perfect . . ."

"Your ballet doesn't need sorting out," Bryony told her firmly. "You're a good dancer!"

Molly sighed. "Just not quite as good as everybody else yet, though, eh?" she said.

"Moll, you're doing great, honestly!" Ellie told her. "Like I said, you've got to cut yourself some slack—it'll take time to catch up." She hoped what she was saying was true. She so wanted Molly to be good enough to stay at The Royal Ballet School!

"Well, I don't think that's how Ms. Black sees it," Molly replied, rolling her eyes. Then she turned away from the mirror and put on her sweat suit top. "Anyway, that's enough moaning. Time to go!"

•   •   •   •

"*Battements fondu* at the barre, please," Ms. Black said crisply, once the girls had all warmed up. "Left foot in *dégagé* second, and raise the foot to 45 degrees . . . and bend the supporting knee, bringing the raised foot to midway between your knee and ankle, keep the working foot nicely pointed, soft easy bend . . . Now straighten both legs together, the working leg lifting *devant*—both legs must straighten together, remember, Molly—and *fondu* again, straighten *à la second.* Is everybody feeling that resistance?"

Ellie and the other girls nodded.

"Good," their teacher said. "Arm up, please, Rebecca—and you, Molly. Like this. Now we'll have four *battements frappe*—front, side, back, side—on each leg. Off you go."

The lesson passed through its usual progression of barre work, followed by *adage* and *allégro* and *port de bras* center work. Ms. Black seemed to be eagle-eyed today, correcting almost everyone. Ellie felt as if she couldn't put so much as a little toe out of place without Ms. Black spotting it!

Poor Molly seemed to be getting the brunt of it, and Ellie could see that, by the end of the class, her friend's shoulders were positively drooping with all the corrections she'd endured. However kind Ms. Black was being—and she *was* correcting Molly in a kindly way each time—Ellie could tell that, as usual, Molly was taking all of the criticisms personally, as if their teacher were attacking her each time rather than trying to help her.

"Thank you very much, everyone," Ms. Black said as the wall clock ticked around to four o'clock.

Ellie, along with the rest of the class, performed the usual reverences to their teacher and the class pianist. And then, as the other girls milled over to the side to pull on their sweat suits, Ellie saw Molly striding across to Ms. Black with a determined look on her face.

"Ms. Black?" Ellie heard her say. "Could I just talk to you about something, please?"

Ms. Black looked down at her watch and shook her head regretfully. "I'm sorry, Molly—I really do have to dash today. I've got to catch a plane to Athens—my sister is getting married there tomorrow, and I'm already cutting it fine. I have to be at London Heathrow Airport in forty minutes, and the traffic is always dreadful on a Friday afternoon. Could it wait until Monday, do you think?"

Molly shrugged. "I guess," she said quietly. And then she straightened her shoulders and put on a bright smile. "Have a great time at your sister's wedding, Ms. Black," she added.

"I will—thanks, Molly," Ms. Black replied, grabbing up her bag and waving at the class pianist. "Good-bye, everyone—see you next week!" she called. And then she hurried out.

Molly stood there for a long moment, and then turned to rejoin Ellie and the other girls. Her eyes were shining with tears.

"Hey! Are you okay?" Ellie asked in concern.

Molly gave her head a small shake, her bottom lip trembling. Then she picked up her things and walked out of the studio.

Ellie, Bryony, and Grace all exchanged glances, and then followed her to the dorm.

There, Molly dropped facedown on her bed. "I give up," she sobbed. "I'm no good. I think I should quit The Royal Ballet School—before they throw me out!"

"Don't say that!" Ellie exclaimed, passing a handful of tissues to her. "Ms. Black was tough on everyone today, not just you."

Molly's tears just kept coming. "I was going to ask Ms. Black if she thinks I should leave," she confessed. "And I never even got the chance to say it, because she had to go. I just feel so . . . so rubbish. I can't do anything right. She watches me like a hawk, and—"

"She watches *everyone* like a hawk," Grace said reassuringly. "That's her job, Molls. She's not picking on you."

"Well, it feels like she is," Molly replied. "Everybody else gets praise—except me. I'm just never good enough. And I hate it! I hate not being good enough—having to be corrected and repositioned every time I do anything!" Her shoulders heaved. "I've tried not to mind, but I do—I really do!" She cried even harder. "I wish I'd never come here!"

Dear Diary,
 Poor Molly! She's just so down on herself

at the moment. It's such a shame that the one day Molly got up the courage to speak to Ms. Black about how she felt, Ms. Black had to rush off and catch a plane.

I wish it were Monday tomorrow, so that Molly could speak to Ms. Black sooner. She says she's seriously thinking about quitting school and going back to Coventry. She wouldn't really do that, would she? I really hope not.

If I'm honest, though, I would hate to be in Molly's shoes, having to catch up with the rest of us. I'm sure Ms. Purvis wouldn't have taken her into the School if she didn't have faith that there was a good chance that Molly could cut it, but . . .

I feel mean to even be writing this down, and I would never, never dream of saying so to Molly but . . . IS she good enough? Will she be able to stay? Ms. Black does seem to correct Molly every two minutes—and now I'm starting to worry about it myself. What if she has to leave, too? I don't think I could bear it if another friend was asked to leave The Royal Ballet School. And Molly would be heartbroken!

A lot of the Year 8 girls seemed to be going home that weekend. Grace was going back to her mom's, as she usually did, and Bryony was going to her grandmother's. Isabelle's dad was over from the States on a rare visit, and had arranged to take her for a day out in London, while Lara had flown home to Dublin, as it was her mom's fortieth birthday party.

"Do you want to go to Richmond? There's a day trip there today," Ellie said to Molly, after the Saturday morning ballet class. Ms. Wells had taken their class that morning, as Ms. Black was away.

Molly shook her head. "Not really," she said. "I just feel like crawling into a cave until Monday, when I can tell Ms. Black how I feel."

"Oh, Moll," Ellie said sympathetically. "You can't do that. Even if there were any caves at Lower School!" Molly gave her a weak smile, and Ellie, feeling encouraged, went on. "I think you need to take a break from worrying this weekend, and have some fun. So why don't we—"

Before Ellie could finish her sentence, Kate's head had popped around the door. "Hi, guys," she said. "Just came to say good-bye before my mum and dad get here—they're taking me out to lunch."

"Nice," Ellie said with a smile. Kate's famous parents were about to open in a series of ballet performances at the Sadlers Wells Theater in London.

Molly looked a little bit starstruck at Kate's news. "You mean Lim Soo May and Christopher Bell are going to be coming *here?*" she asked, wide-eyed. "In this building?"

Kate nodded and smiled. "In this building, yes," she confirmed. "Come and meet them, if you want," she added. "They're due here in a few minutes."

A wondrous smile lit up Molly's face, chasing away the misery that had been in her eyes for the last hour or so. "Seriously? You mean it?" she breathed. "You'll actually *introduce* me to them?"

"Sure," Kate said, "as long as you promise to introduce me to your parents next time they're here," she added. "Because I know Mum and Chris are famous and everything, but they're still just people, like everyone else's parents."

"Well, actually they're just a *teeny* bit more exciting than my mum and dad," Molly said, laughing. "If I even dare imagine my mum and dad in leotards, leaping about a stage in the West End . . ." She began jumping clumsily around the dorm in an imitation that left Ellie and Kate helpless with giggles.

"Stop, Moll," Ellie laughed as Molly blundered through a pirouette, almost falling over one of the beds as she went on clowning. "I'll never be able to look at your mom again without thinking of you doing this now!"

Molly curtsied inelegantly and grinned. "And that's Coventry's finest, Nigel and Cath Baker, performing Sleeping Beauty's Worst Nightmare!" she said, in a cheesy announcer's voice. "Maybe I should perform it in front of your parents, Kate?"

Kate grinned back at her. "I'll hold you to that," she said. "Come on, let's see if they've arrived yet. You could dance in reception for them, if you want."

Molly shook her head and laughed. "Not likely," she said lightly. "If Ms. Black thinks I've got a lot to learn, your parents will probably be shocked if they saw me really dancing. What *has* happened to The Royal Ballet School's standards?" she added in a disapproving-sounding voice.

Kate elbowed her playfully as they made their way out of the dorm. "As if!" she snorted. "My parents would say nothing of the sort. They know how hard we all work here."

"And how good we all are, too," Ellie said forcefully. There went Molly, putting herself down again. "Every last one of us!"

"Yeah, well . . ." Molly muttered as they walked along the corridor.

A smile broke out over Kate's face as they walked into the foyer area. "Hi, Chris!" she called out, spotting a tall, handsome man leaning on the front desk, chatting to Diane, the receptionist there. Then she frowned. "Where's Mum?"

"Oh, my gosh!" Molly squeaked, flushing at the sight of the

famous dancer. "It really is him!"

Christopher Bell smiled and strolled over toward the girls. "Hi, Katie," he said, hugging her. "Your mum's still at the theater. She said for us to meet her there, if that's okay." His eyes fell upon the other two girls. "Hello—Ellie, isn't it? And hi there," he said to Molly, "I don't think we've met before."

"Hello again," Ellie said, feeling a little shy at being so close to a superstar. She'd met him a couple of times now, but she still felt completely in awe of him.

"Oh, sorry—Chris, this is Molly," Kate said. "She's new at Lower School."

"Um . . . hi," Molly said breathlessly. "I feel as if I should be curtsying in front of you or something. I am so excited about meeting you!"

Christopher laughed good-naturedly. "Very nice to meet you too, Molly," he said.

"Please do tell Lim Soo May what a big fan I am," Molly said. "I just think she is sooo wonderful. I mean, one of the greatest. Maybe *the* greatest! I mean . . ." After Molly's initial shyness, it seemed as if she couldn't stop talking now, Ellie thought in amusement.

"Well, you can tell her yourself, if you want to," Christopher said, with a smile. "If you and Ellie don't have anything better to do, you can come along—Soo May did say I should ask any of Kate's friends to join us, too, if they wanted." He turned to Kate. "She was really looking forward to coming into the school to see your friends, Kate, and she's sorry that she couldn't make it today."

Kate looked at Ellie and Molly. "What do you reckon, then, girls? Fancy coming into London for a spot of lunch?" She lowered her voice to a stage whisper. "Please say you will. If Mum's still rehearsing, I might get bored if I'm stuck with Chris all on my own."

Chris laughed at Kate's cheek. "Hey! I heard that!"

"I'd *love* to come," Ellie said at once. She couldn't believe her luck! What an unexpected treat! She pulled her cell phone out of her pocket. "I'll just phone my mom to check if it's okay—but there's *no way* she'll say no. Not if she ever wants me to speak to her again, that is!"

"And I'd love to come, too," Molly said, looking absolutely dazzled. "Are you sure that's okay? I won't be in the way or anything?"

"Not at all," Chris said warmly. "Any friend of Kate's is a friend of ours. Isn't that right, Kate?"

"Right," Kate said, taking a cell phone out of her jacket pocket. "Here, borrow this to call your mum if you want, Molly."

Ellie's mom said yes immediately, of course. Ellie whooped with joy.

Molly was still on the phone to her mom. "No, really, it's not a joke," she was saying, rolling her eyes. She covered up the mouthpiece and pulled a comic face at the others. "She thinks I'm trying to wind her up!" she whispered. "No, Mum—seriously. I'm asking seriously—I need to get your permission to go, and—"

"May I?" Christopher asked, holding his hand out for the phone.

Molly giggled and handed it over.

"Hello—Mrs. Baker?" Christopher asked in his deep voice. "This is Christopher Bell . . . yes, *the* Christopher Bell. I—"

The scream of excitement from the other end of the phone was so loud, Christopher had to take the phone away from his ear. "Your mum's got a good set of lungs on her," he joked to Molly, who was squirming with embarrassment.

"You're telling me," she muttered. "Can I speak to her again?" Chris passed the phone back, and Molly spoke into it. "Yes, it *was* him. No, I *won't* wait while you put Dad on to listen!"

Kate and Ellie burst out laughing. This phone call was turning into quite a saga!

"Right—okay, that's great," Molly said, sounding relieved. "No, I won't get you an autograph! Oh, honestly, Mum—you're really embarrassing me—he's standing right here!" she hissed. "Okay—yes, I'll call you later. No, don't call me. Whatever you do, don't call me!"

She pressed the "end" button on Kate's phone and passed it back to her. "What is she like?" she groaned. "A one-woman embarrassment show, that's what." She grinned at them all. "Anyway, she said yes. Finally! So I'll just run and get my jacket . . ."

"Me too," Ellie said. "We'll be back in five!"

"Great," Chris said. "We'll be in the car right outside."

Ellie and Molly raced back to the dorm.

"I think I might faint with excitement!" Molly gasped. "I can't believe we're actually going into London to have lunch with Lim Soo May and Christopher Bell!" She practically screamed their names out, and some of the Year 9 boys, who were going the opposite way, looked at them very strangely.

"I know," Ellie said, feeling giddy at the thought. "This sure beats going on a trip to Richmond, any day!"

•   •   •   •

Ellie, Molly, Kate, and Chris arrived at the Sadlers Wells Theater an hour or so later.

"Hopefully, Soo May will have finished by now," Chris said as he led them through the labyrinth of corridors backstage. "She was just practicing the final movements with the director, so fingers crossed, she'll be showered and ready to grab some lunch soon."

He knocked on a dressing room door that had his and Soo May's name on it, then peeked around it. "Hmm, she's not there," he said. "Let's see what's happening on the stage."

Molly looked as if she were in a daze as Chris led them to the stage. Ellie felt pretty overwhelmed, too. She kept wanting to pinch herself just to make sure she wasn't dreaming. Not only was she in the famous Sadlers Wells Theater, she was also with the amazing Christopher Bell and about to join him and the equally amazing Lim Soo May for lunch! Even if it *was* a dream, dreams didn't get much better than this!

Kate was the only one of them who was trotting along behind Chris as if this was an everyday occurrence. Ellie simply couldn't imagine ever feeling so nonchalant about it.

"Oh, here she is," Chris said as he led them out into an area in front of the stage. "Are you all done here?"

Soo May was looking rather flustered, Ellie couldn't help thinking, as she smiled up at the pretty ballerina on stage.

"Not quite," Soo May called down. "Hi Katie, hi girls." She threw her hands up in the air, with an exasperated look on her face. "I feel as if I'm *never* going to be done today. I just can't get this movement right. I'm no good at all!"

A short, muscular-looking man nodded a greeting to Chris and Kate, and then turned to his principal dancer. "Come on, Soo May, we've already talked about this," he said firmly. "Of course you can do it! I know you can—and *you* know you can."

Soo May heaved out a huge sigh. "I don't think so," she said, a worried look crossing her face. "I've lost it. I've got a real block about this movement. I'll never be able to get it."

The director folded his arms across his chest. "You know, I remember you saying those exact same words when you were dancing Aurora for me, the first time I cast you in *Sleeping Beauty*. And look at you now—it's your most famous part!" His voice was stern, but Ellie could see that his eyes were soft as he went on: "I know you hate it when you feel like you haven't quite mastered something, but I also know—and *you* know, too—that going over and over and *over* the steps is the only way you're going to perfect them, and feel comfortable with them."

"I know, but—" Soo May began protesting, but the director waved her words aside with his hand.

"Let's stop talking about it, anyway. These girls look like they want some lunch. Are you going to keep them here, starving hungry, while we argue about it?" he said.

"No, but I—" Soo May began, but the director simply held up his arm.

Music began to play again. "Then dance," he told her. "Let's get it right before we break for lunch."

"We'll *all* be starving by the time I get it right," Ellie heard Soo May grumble in a low voice, but she obediently went to stand on her mark while she waited for her cue.

Kate sat down in one of the theater seats. "We might be here a while if Mum's having one of her wobbly days," she whispered to Ellie and Molly. "Might as well make ourselves comfortable and watch a bit of the show, eh?"

"Wobbly days?" Molly queried as the music started and Soo May began practicing her steps up on the stage.

Kate nodded. "She always has a wobble before a big show: She can't do it—she's lost her touch—she's going to let all her fans down," she said casually, her eyes on her mother the whole time. "Every time. But when it's showtime . . . she does it."

"And she does it brilliantly," Chris said loyally, watching his wife.

"She *is* brilliant," Ellie breathed, feeling in awe all over again as she watched Soo May make the stage her own, leaping across it with the lightest of touches. "I can't believe she'd ever think otherwise."

"Nor me," Molly whispered. "I mean—look at her. She's a prima ballerina. She's incredible. And to think she still struggles with a new move!"

Ellie took her eyes off the stage for a second and saw a grin break over Molly's face.

"There's hope for me yet," Molly hissed in delight.

Up on stage, Soo May was finishing the movement—and smiling.

"Better—so much better!" the director called out encouragingly. "Did it feel different to you?"

"Yes," Soo May said happily. "I feel like I'm close to getting it, after all." She smiled down at Kate. "Maybe I won't be out of a job just yet."

"And maybe you should have your lunch now, eh? Finish on a high note," the director said. He went over and hugged her, then checked his watch. "I'll see you back here in an hour and a half, yes?" he said. "You're doing great."

Soo May hurried off for a quick shower, emerging a few minutes later looking radiant and happy, in a pale pink sweat suit. "Hello, sweetheart," she said, throwing her arms around Kate.

Kate introduced Molly to her mom, and Molly managed to splutter out a near-breathless hello and bob a little curtsy. "You don't have to curtsy to my *mum*," Kate said, laughing.

"Kate, don't tease her," Soo May said, linking an arm through Molly's. "So, you're new, are you?" she asked as they went out of the theater and into a small French restaurant nearby. "How are you finding life at The Royal Ballet School?"

"Well," Molly said, less shy now, "hard work, to be honest." She started telling Soo May about the problems she'd been experiencing as they sat down at a table in a quiet corner of the restaurant. Then suddenly she shook her head. "Gosh, sorry," she gasped, looking appalled. "I can't believe I'm sitting with you two megastars, and I'm just complaining on and on about my little problems!"

Soo May and Chris smiled at each other.

"Molly, what you've been describing is something that goes on and on in ballet; the constant struggle for perfection is what all dancers share—even ballerinas," Soo May said gently. "Take me, for instance—I have been dancing those steps all morning, it seems. The same movement, over and over again. You saw for yourself, I was finding it really difficult. And I was grateful that the director pushed me so hard. That's what ballet is all about—pushing on, constantly striving for perfection, even when you sometimes doubt your ability. And Molly, we all battle against our insecurity."

Chris was nodding. "So you really should take heart from the fact that Ms. Black is pushing *you* all the time." He smiled warmly at Molly. "The director whom you saw just now—he's a terrible one for criticizing his dancers, you know."

"Really?" Molly asked.

"Really," Soo May and Chris chorused fervently.

"He's had me in tears many times before," Soo May said.

"And I've definitely felt like throwing my ballet shoes at him more than once!" Chris chuckled.

Ellie giggled, finding it hard to imagine easygoing Chris losing his temper with anybody.

"But we love him for it, too," Soo May went on, "because, by pushing, pushing, pushing, he gets the best out of us."

Molly was nodding slowly. "I suppose if you look at it that way, it *is* good to be corrected," she said. "Even if it doesn't feel like it at the time."

"Absolutely," Chris said. Then he picked up a handful of menus and handed them around. "Now, then," he said, "what are all you brilliant ballerinas going to have for lunch?"

Dear Diary
   What an awesome day! It was so amazing to watch Lim Soo May prepare for her performance tonight—wow! She was even better than I remember her, and just so friendly. I still can't believe she's Kate's mom sometimes. It seems too much like a fairytale!
   Chris is great, too. He had us all roaring with laughter over lunch, with his

impressions of the rest of the cast. Once Molly had gotten over being starstruck, she joined in, doing impressions of the waiter who was serving us in the restaurant. I laughed so much, I thought I was going to fall off my chair.

Molly also had a really fantastic day. She was sooo excited about meeting Kate's parents—she's been on the phone to her mom, dad, grandmother, and about twenty of her friends, telling them all about it. But the best thing of all was seeing her face as she realized that even a ballerina like Lim Soo May could experience the same problems that she's going through. She's been a different person ever since—happier than I've seen her for a long time. Molly's got her bounce back again—hooray!!

Chapter 9

The following Monday, after ballet class had ended, Ellie followed Grace and the others back up to the dorm to shower and change for tuck, leaving Molly deep in conversation with their teacher. Though Molly had felt so much better after Soo May and Christopher's encouraging words on Saturday, she had still wanted to hear what Ms. Black truly felt about her dancing.

As she rinsed the shampoo suds from her hair, Ellie wondered anxiously how Molly was getting on. She so wanted her new friend to stay on at The Royal Ballet School—and she desperately wanted Ms. Black to be positive toward Molly. She'd only been a student here a few weeks—yet, already, Ellie couldn't imagine Lower School without bubbly, fun-loving Molly.

She didn't have too long to wait. She'd only just sat down with a drink of juice when Molly appeared in the canteen, with a big smile on her face.

"Everything okay?" Ellie asked.

"More than okay," Molly said happily. "Ms. Black was soooo nice. She said she's been really impressed by all my hard work and determination—oops, let me just polish my halo!"

Ellie laughed as Molly started rubbing a pretend halo above her head. "Fantastic," she said. "Well done. What else?"

Molly leaned back in her chair. "She was actually surprised that I'd been doubting myself. She—" Molly broke off, suddenly looking a little embarrassed. "Hey, I don't want to sound like I'm blowing my own trumpet but . . ."

"Oh, blow it, girl, blow it," Bryony said, joining the conversation.

"Well, okay, she said I'd exceeded all her expectations so far," Molly went on, "and she said she knew she'd been pushing me hard, but it's only because she has faith in me."

"What did we tell you!" Ellie said, grinning across the table at her.

"And I told her that I'd been thinking maybe I should drop out of Lower School," Molly said, "and Ms. Black's mouth just sort of fell open, like this—"

"Very attractive," Lara said, giggling as Molly's jaw practically hit the table.

"And she was really, *really* insistent about how I should stay, because I'm . . . well, good enough to stay, and—" Molly broke off, rather flushed. "Anyway, that's enough about how great I am. I'll save the rest to tell my mum."

"Oh, Moll, that's brilliant. You must feel so much better about being here now," Ellie said warmly. Secretly, she felt hugely relieved, too, after her own recent doubts about Molly. "And quite right, too."

"I do, I do," Molly said. "I feel so happy, I can't tell you. I was really getting to think that Ms. Black had it in for me . . ."

"Rubbish," Grace snorted.

"And now I feel like she's on my side," Molly finished, with a relieved sigh. "I can cope with anything now. Even"—she lowered her voice as she looked around to check who was within earshot—"even dancing with Oliver in character class for the rest of the term!"

Lara raised her eyebrows. "Well, if you're really lucky, Molls, you'll get to dance with him at the school disco on Friday night, too," she said, chuckling.

The disco that Lara was referring to was something that everyone was looking forward to. A group of the older students had asked permission to have one on the penultimate Friday before half-term—and, as Mr. Whitehouse had offered to oversee the whole thing, Ms. Purvis had agreed.

•   •   •   •

When Friday came around, everybody was in a partying mood. Ellie and her friends all rushed through supper and prep so that they would have maximum time to get ready in the dorm.

"What do you think? Does this green top make my face look a weird color?" Molly asked, a dubious expression on her face.

Ellie laughed at the question. "No," she assured her. "That color looks really good on you, actually. And I love those white pants you're wearing."

Molly frowned. "What?" she exclaimed. "No! Don't tell me you can see my knickers through these trousers!"

Ellie roared with laughter as Molly twisted this way and that in front of the mirror, trying to see if her underwear was visible.

"Sorry," Ellie said. "I'm speaking American. I mean, I love your white *trousers*. Trousers—pants—same thing to me, okay?"

Molly grinned. "Phew!" she said. "That's okay then. So, I'm glad you like my white *pants*, Ell!"

"I wish I could decide what to wear," Bryony said, trying on her fourth outfit in as many minutes.

"Well, I *have* decided what to wear—but now I've got a jewelry dilemma," Grace wailed. "Necklace *and* bracelet, or just necklace?" she wondered aloud. "Or just bracelet? Or no jewelry at all? Oh, help! Where's my personal stylist when I need her?"

"Same place as mine—in our imaginations, unfortunately," Bryony said. She twirled around in a rose-pink T-shirt and black jeans. "What do you think? Too casual? Too scruffy?"

"Nice," Grace said approvingly. "The boys will love it."

Bryony blushed. "Any boys in particular, or just all of them?" she asked.

"Oh, all of them, I should think," Grace replied. "Why, *is* there anyone in particular that you're wondering about?"

"No, not really," Bryony said. She glanced at her reflection in the mirror and then pulled the T-shirt off her head in one movement. "Actually, it *is* too casual, I think," she said. "No, I mean, some of the Year 9 boys are cute—like Tom and Joshua—but I'd never dare go and ask them to dance or anything." She went back to her wardrobe and started rummaging through it again. "I'd be so embarrassed, I don't think I could get the words out!" She pulled out a turquoise halter-neck top and slipped it off the hanger. "Ahh—this is more like it. How about you guys, anyway? Any secret crushes going on that I don't know about?"

Ellie could feel Molly's eyes upon her and busied herself with her hair. "Is that the time already?" she said quickly, in order to avoid answering Bryony's question. She didn't want to tell anyone about her feelings for Luke, in case it got back to him. "Help! The disco starts in ten minutes and I'm not even dressed!"

•   •   •   •

The disco was taking place in the Margot Fonteyn Studio, one of the largest practice studios. Mr. Whitehouse and a team of helpers had strung up colorful lights from the ceiling and set up the sound system. There was also a refreshment stand, which was being manned by volunteer students. Ellie knew that Alice had offered to do a stint on it, as had Luke. She cursed herself for not putting her name down to help out, too. If she'd only known that Luke was going to be at the stand, she definitely would have volunteered, too. And now, chances were, Luke and Alice would be together—again!

One of the older girls, Thea, was acting as DJ for the evening, and was playing some brilliant music as Ellie and her friends arrived. Ellie couldn't stop her eyes scanning the crowd for a glimpse of Luke. Aha! There he was behind the counter at the refreshment stand. Right next to Alice.

"Just going to grab a drink," Ellie said breezily. "It's hot in here. Anybody else want anything?"

"Not for me," Molly replied. "Oh, I love this song! Let's go and dance!"

As her friends rushed onto the dance floor, Ellie headed off to the drinks stand. As she approached, she could see Luke and Alice laughing together about something.

Ellie felt her heart twist, but marched purposefully on. "Hi, guys," she said as she reached the stand. "Lemonade, please."

"Hi, Ellie," Luke said, pouring some into a paper cup. He passed it to Ellie, and she almost flinched as his fingers brushed against hers, making them tingle. "You look nice," he added with a smile.

"Oh, thanks," Ellie replied, trying to sound casual, but secretly thrilled. *Nicer than Alice?* she wanted to ask. She closed her mouth hurriedly before the words could get out.

"Come on, Ellie!" came Lara's voice from the dance floor. "Come and dance!"

Ellie turned. *I'm just standing here chatting with Luke,* she wanted to say—but then Oliver Stafford came up to the refreshment stand, and loudly began to tell Luke a joke he'd just heard. The moment was lost.

Sighing inwardly, Ellie drained her paper cup and tossed it in the trash. "Okay!" she called to Lara, and began to make her way over to the dance floor.

Ellie danced for a couple more songs with the girls, and then a slower song came on that she wasn't so keen on. "I'm going to sit this one out," she called, and headed over to the side, where a couple of tables and chairs had been set up.

She decided she'd sit down and sneak a few peeks over at Luke and Alice, just to check out what they were doing. But when she looked over at the refreshment stand, she saw that Scarlett and Danny were behind the counter now. Luke and Alice had gone.

Gone where? Gone somewhere together?

"Hi there," came a voice just then. "Mind if I join you?"

Ellie looked up to see Luke standing next to her. Alone. "Sure," she said, her heart doing a flip.

"I was just wondering if you were okay," he began, his blue eyes looking concerned, "with Matt dancing with Kate so much."

Ellie felt puzzled and looked over toward the dance floor where Matt was spinning Kate around. "Oh—I hadn't noticed," she said, wondering why Luke was mentioning it to her.

"I mean, I know you two are . . . well . . ." Luke said, stumbling over the words.

Ellie felt even more puzzled. "What? Me and Matt? We're just friends," she said. "Why, did you think . . . ? Did you think we were an item?"

Luke nodded. "Well, you seem to spend a lot of time together."

"As friends, yes," Ellie told him quickly. "But nothing else."

Luke gave a little laugh, suddenly looking sheepish. "Well, I'm glad," he said. "Because . . ."

Ellie's heart was pounding now. Why was Luke taking such an interest? Surely it couldn't be because . . . she hardly dared finish the thought.

"Ahh, there you are, Luke!"

Ellie looked up to see Alice standing in front of them. "Can I tear him away from you, Ellie?" she asked. "Scarlett and Danny are run off their feet over there—I said we'd go back and help."

Luke turned back to Ellie. "Sorry," he said. "Can we catch up later?"

"Of course," Ellie replied. She watched him go back over to the refreshment stand, and suddenly she felt giddy. What had Luke been about to *say?* Oh, why had Alice turned up just at that very second?!

"I saw you talking to Luke," Molly said, coming and sitting down next to her just then. "Is everything all right?"

"I think so," Ellie replied, fanning herself with her hand. It was so hot in there all of a sudden!

"Tell me," Molly urged. "You like him, don't you? What was he saying?"

Ellie's eyes drifted away toward Luke. She bit her lip, weighing whether or not to divulge her precious secret. But Molly was a good friend, wasn't she? And she was desperate to tell *someone!* "Promise you won't say anything?" she asked hesitantly.

Molly nodded.

"Well, I do kind of like him. There—I said it." Ellie's heart was thumping as she said the words. Her secret was out—not that she'd been able to keep it very well hidden from Molly! "But he just told me now that he's been thinking all along that me and Matt were an item—when we're really not. And when I said that Matt and I are just friends, he said he was glad, because . . ."

"Because what?" Molly asked, her eyes bright.

"Well, that's the problem," Ellie groaned. "He was just about to say why, when Alice popped up and asked him to go back on the drinks stand with her. So he never got to finish his sentence—and now the moment's totally gone!" Ellie sighed. "And, anyway, I think he prefers Alice. Look at them," she added mournfully.

Molly followed Ellie's gaze, to where Alice and Luke were clowning around together behind the drinks counter. And then she pulled Ellie to her feet. "Come on, come and dance again. Take your mind off it all, with a good boogie."

"Okay," Ellie said, but her heart wasn't really in it. How she wished Luke hadn't been interrupted just then!

Dear Diary,

The suspense is killing me! It was such a tease, hearing Luke saying what he did—and then not getting a single chance to be alone with him for the rest of the evening so he could finish what he was saying.

It is so frustrating!

I won't get to see him all weekend now,

either, because I heard him say that he's going off to some family party straight after ballet class tomorrow. And then it'll be the last week of term, and there's always so much going on that I'll probably never get to speak to him.

Aaargggh! It's enough to drive a girl crazy!

Chapter 10

It was the last day before half-term, and for their Friday morning geography lesson, Ellie's class had come into Richmond on a field trip to look at local amenities. They'd prepared a questionnaire in the previous class and were going to use it to interview passersby to find out what they thought about the shops, the bus service, the information signs, and so on.

Mr. Whitehouse led the class to Richmond's elegant green, just off the high street, and assembled them in front of the library. "Right, class, can you organize yourselves into teams of four, please?" he instructed.

To Ellie's surprise, Molly grabbed her by the hand and dragged her over to where Matt and Luke were standing. "There—we four can go together," she said decisively.

Ellie was a little taken aback by Molly's swiftness, but smiled at the boys. "Fine with me," she said.

"Now, everyone. I want you all back here at twelve o'clock, sharp—okay? We can't afford to hang around—otherwise, you'll be late for lunch."

"Ahhh, sir—can't we have lunch here in Richmond?" Danny

called out with a cheeky grin.

Mr. Whitehouse pretended to mop his brow. "Danny," he said, "are you prepared to face Mrs. Garrett in the canteen and tell her you don't want the special 'last Friday' lunch she's slaved over a hot stove to cook for you? Because I'm scared of her, even if you're not."

Everyone laughed.

"So, twelve sharp it is, then," Mr. Whitehouse repeated as the teams began dispersing. "And stick together!"

"Sir, can we stay here at the green?" Matt asked. "There are loads of people around here we could ask."

"Good idea, Matt," Mr. Whitehouse replied. "Good luck!"

Soon the other students had all moved off, leaving only Ellie's group in the green.

"Right, here's the plan," said Matt. "We get our surveys done really fast, so that we've got a bit of free time afterward. Everyone agree?"

"Definitely," Ellie said. "We need twenty surveys done, don't we? And if we do it in pairs, we'll be done twice as quickly." She glanced around. Leading off the green were a couple of cobbled lanes full of boutiques and cafés. "Maybe Molly and I could stand at the entrance of one of the lanes while you two stay on the green. That way, we'd still be within sight of one another."

"Good call, Ellie," said Luke.

"Okay," Matt agreed. "So it's boys against girls—let's see who finishes their ten first!"

Molly linked arms with Ellie as they went off together. "He likes you," she whispered in Ellie's ear.

"What? Who?" Ellie replied, feeling flustered.

"What, who, indeed!" Molly said, mock-severely. "Like you don't know who I'm talking about. Luke, of course! Your blue-eyed boy!"

"Do you think so?" Ellie asked, her heart fluttering at her friend's words.

"Actually . . . I *know* so . . ." Molly said. "Matt told me. Ahh, excuse me, sir," she said, breaking off suddenly and waving at an elderly gentleman in front of them. "Would you mind answering a few questions, please?" She gave her most winning smile. "We're doing a little survey—it'll only take a minute . . ."

Ellie had to hand it to her friend: Molly was so good at sweet-talking potential interviewees that nobody refused her. Unfortunately, that meant that they were going from one questionnaire to another—with not a minute in between for Ellie to interrogate Molly further on what she'd just told her!

She felt as if she were going through the questionnaires in a daze. *Luke likes me! Matt had said so!* She could hardly believe it.

"So when did Matt tell you?" she managed to hiss, after they'd completed their fourth survey. "And what did he say?"

"He told me this morning, in history," Molly told her. "He'd borrowed a book from Luke and he said a picture of you fell out of it when he opened it up. A picture Luke had cut out of the school magazine!"

"No!" Ellie gasped, her hands flying up to her cheeks. She couldn't help glancing across at Luke. Her heart melted at the lovely smile he gave the little old lady he and Matt were questioning.

"Oh yes," Molly replied, grinning. "So Matt asked Luke if he liked you, and Luke said yes, and . . . oh! Excuse me, madam!"

"Moll—finish what you were saying!" Ellie begged as Molly started waving at an old lady who was coming toward them. But Molly was already beaming at the old lady and asking her to answer a few questions. "Only short questions, I promise," she said.

"For a lovely, polite girl like you, of course I'll do your survey," the old lady said. "Beautiful manners, dear! You don't see that very often these days . . ."

After the old lady came a young mum with twin babies, then they interviewed a friendly man with his dog. And before Ellie knew it, they'd completed ten surveys—and she still hadn't gotten the full story from Molly.

"Quick—here come the boys. Tell me what else Matt said," she hissed.

"Matt said Luke should ask you out," Molly said. "And Luke said—"

"We've done our ten!" Matt shouted at that moment, waving a fist full of completed questionnaires above his head as he and Luke walked up to them.

"So have we," Molly said, holding up theirs.

Ellie was so excited, she could hardly bring herself to look at Luke. He liked her! Luke really liked her!

"Excellent," Matt said, stuffing his questionnaires into his rucksack. "And it's only twenty-five past eleven. We are champion surveyors!"

"So we've got half an hour to ourselves," Luke said. He smiled at Ellie.

"Molly—I was wondering, would you come and help me choose a CD for my brother?" Matt said. "I know that you're really into your music, so . . ." He linked arms with Molly and started pulling her away. "We'll see you guys later!" he called over his shoulder. "We're just going into the music shop over there, okay?" he said, pointing into one of the lanes leading off the green.

Ellie felt a little flustered. She and Luke had so obviously been set up by Matt and Molly! Suddenly she didn't know what to say.

"Fancy a stroll around the green?" Luke asked. "There are some really amazing houses around it."

"Good idea," she replied, grateful for the suggestion.

"I—" Ellie began, and then she jumped as Luke slipped his hand into hers as they began to walk. "You're holding my hand!" she blurted out—and then the blood surged into her cheeks as she realized she'd just spoken her thoughts aloud.

Luke smiled at her. "Is that all right?" he asked.

Ellie nodded, her heart thumping. She couldn't speak, she felt so overwhelmed. She was walking along with Luke, and they were holding hands! Actually holding hands!

"Good," Luke went on casually as if this were a quite natural occurrence. "Because I was wondering . . . would you go out with me?"

"Go out with you?" Ellie echoed, mystified as to what he meant. "We're already out, aren't we?"

Luke laughed. He'd gone a little red. "It's a British expression," he explained, dropping his gaze from Ellie's and looking a bit shy all of a sudden. "Going out with someone—it means being . . . boyfriend and girlfriend."

Ellie smiled up at him. "You mean—you're asking me to be your girlfriend?" She had to stop herself from jumping up and down, she was so delirious at the thought.

Luke groaned. "Ellie, don't make me say it all over again!" Then he turned to her with a smile and said, "Okay, as it's you— Ellie Brown, will you be my girlfriend?"

"Yes!" Ellie replied, her voice coming out in a squeak. "Oh, I've been hoping and hoping you'd ask me since the beginning of term—" She put her hand up to her mouth, not sure if she was gushing too much.

Luke laughed. "I've been *wanting* to, but I thought you and Matt—"

"And I thought you and Alice—" Ellie interrupted. A happy feeling was bubbling up inside her at this amazing conversation.

"Me and Alice? No—we're just friends, same as you and Matt," Luke said. He squeezed her hand. "I'm glad we got that straight at last!"

"Oh, me too!" Ellie said fervently. "After that Irish dancing class, when we were partners, I so wanted to dance with you again, but then Matt asked me, and I didn't want to hurt his feelings and—"

Ellie couldn't say any more, because Luke was kissing her. She stood there, her heart thumping, blood rushing around her whole body. His lips were so soft on hers, and she could smell a faint soapy scent on his face. Luke! She was being kissed by Luke! Ellie had never been kissed by a boy before. She had never in a zillion years imagined it would be quite so nice. She felt as if her insides were melting.

Luke pulled away, but his arms were still around her. "I hate to say this, but we'd better go back," he murmured. "We don't want Mr. Whitehouse to leave us in the wilds of Richmond, all alone."

"Are you sure?" Ellie asked, smiling up at him. "I wouldn't mind."

Luke kissed her again, this time on the forehead, and tucked a strand of her hair behind her ears. "You're lovely," he said. "I've wanted to do that for so long."

"I'm so glad you did," Ellie said. "But I'm going to spend the whole of half term week back home in Oxford, missing you," she added, a little sorrowfully. She could hardly bear it—they'd only just gotten together, and tomorrow they were going to be apart for a whole week for the mid-semester break. It was going to seem like the longest week in history!

"Me too," Luke said as they began strolling back the way they'd come, still hand in hand. "But we can swap phone numbers and e-mail addresses . . . hey, if you're lucky, I might even write you a letter."

Ellie grinned. "And then when we're back at school again, we can carry on where we just left off," she said. "I can't wait!"

Dear Diary,
  Guess what!
  I've got a boyfriend!
  What a way to end the first half of term! Luke Bailey is my boyfriend! He liked me all along, too. I can hardly believe it! I feel sooo happy!
  Molly just screamed with excitement when I told her. "I knew it! I knew it!" she kept saying.
  He is just soooo gorgeous! And funny. And, oh, such a nice kisser . . . I feel like I just want to be with him all the time. I want to know EVERYTHING about him!
  It's going to be torture, tearing myself away from him tomorrow to go home.
  This evening has been really nice. Us four "Room-Off" girls have been hanging out in our pj's, packing up our things and talking

about everything. And Bryony gave Molly a pair of ballet shoes she'd embroidered especially for her—because Molly had missed out on the tradition, coming to school a bit late.

Molly was so thrilled and touched, I thought she was going to cry. Then she made us all laugh by doing her "mom dance" in them—we had to beg her to stop because by then I was almost crying—with laughter!

So far, Year 8 has been memorable, to say the least! I just can't wait to see what's going to happen in the rest of it!

GLOSSARY

ROYAL BALLET METHOD: An eight-year system of training and methodology developed and utilized by The Royal Ballet School to produce dancers with clean, pure classical technique

ADAGE: From the musical direction *adagio,* meaning slow; slow work with emphasis on sustained positions and on balance

ALLÉGRO, GRAND ALLÉGRO, PETIT ALLÉGRO: Jumps that can be performed at various speeds

ARABESQUE: One leg is extended to the back (the name is taken from the flourished, curved line used in Arabic motifs)

ATTITUDE: *Grande pose;* one leg in the air with the knee bent either to the front or back

BALANCÉ: To rock; a swinging three-step movement transferring weight from one foot to the other

BALLONNÉ: Jumping step during which the dancer stretches one leg to the front or back, landing on the other leg with the stretched leg returning to *coup-de-pied* on closing

BARRE: The horizontal wooden bar fastened to the walls of the ballet classroom or rehearsal hall that the dancer holds for support

BATTEMENT: To beat; a beating of the legs; see *grand battement, petit battement,* and *battement frappé* for variations

BATTEMENT FONDU: To melt; a movement on one leg, bending and extending both legs at the same time

BATTEMENT FRAPPÉ: To strike; a striking action of the working foot

BATTU: To beat; an adjective to describe a beat of the feet; the term is always added on to a step to describe the additional movement, for example *changement battu*

BOURRÉE: A series of running steps that can be done on *demi-pointe* but more frequently on full *pointe*

BRAS BAS: The rounding of the arms held in front of the thighs with a small space between the hands

CHASSÉ (ALSO PAS CHASSÉ): A gliding step when the leg slides out and the other leg is drawn along the floor to it

COUP DE PIED: Around the "neck" of the foot; one pointed foot is placed at the calf—just above the ankle—of the opposite leg

CROISÉ: To cross; a diagonal position with one leg crossed in front of the other

DEMI-PLIÉ: A small bend (of the knees) in alignment over the toes, without causing the heel, or heels, of the foot to lift off the floor

DEMI-POINTE: Rising *en pointe* only halfway, onto the ball of the foot, not completely onto the toes

DEVANT: In front; a step, movement or the placing of an arm or leg in front of the body

DEVELOPPÉ: The unfolding of the working leg; the leg is drawn to the knee and then extended from there

ECHAPPÉ: To escape (a movement that begins in 5th position and moves quickly to 2nd position either by sliding to the ball of the foot or as a jump from 5th position to 2nd position)

EN CROIX: In the form of a cross; a four-step movement that begins from a closed position and takes the leg to the front, side, back, and side again

EN DEDANS: Inward; indicates the direction of the working leg (counterclockwise) or the pirouette (toward the supporting leg)

EN DEHORS: Outward; indicates the direction of the leg (clockwise) or the direction of the supporting leg during a pirouette (toward the outer leg)

ENTRECHAT: A jump from two feet, crossing the feet rapidly in the air and landing either on one (if an odd number of crossings) or two feet (if an even number)

FONDU: To melt (bending and extending of the legs at the same time with one leg supporting the body)

FOUETTÉ: To whip; a quick movement on one leg that requires the dancer to change direction and can be performed in a variety of ways

GLISSADE: To glide; a connecting step that begins and ends in *plié*

GRAND BATTEMENT: A throwing action of the fully extended leg in any direction with controlled lowering

GRAND JETÉ: A throwing action; a high jump from one foot to the other

GRAND PLIÉ: A deeper bend (of the knees) bringing the heels of the feet off the floor

JETÉ: A jump from one foot to the other

PAS DE BOURRÉE: A linking movement done as a series of three quick, small steps

PAS DE BOURREÉ PIQUÉ: *Piqué* means "to prick"; a quick step out on one leg to the half-toe or *pointe* position during *pas de bourrée*

PAS DE CHAT: Cat's step (because the movement is like a cat's leap); a jump where the legs are lifted and lowered separately, forming a diamond shape in the air

PETIT BATTEMENT: Small beat whereby a pointed foot "beats" in front and back of the calf—just above the ankle—of the opposite leg; this exercise is done with great rapidity

PETIT BATTERIE: A general term to describe a beating of the legs

PIROUETTE: Turn (used to describe a turn, whirl, or spin); "turns" are sometimes referred to as *tours*

PLIÉ: To bend (the knee or knees)

PORT DE BRAS: Carriage of the arms; specific movements of the upper torso and arms

POINTE: "Going *en pointe*" is to graduate from soft ballet shoes to the more demanding pointe shoes that have a hard box at the toe in the shape of a cone onto which the tips of the toes balance

RELEVÉ: To rise (used to describe a rise from the whole foot to *demi-pointe* or full *pointe*)

RETIRÉ: To withdraw (drawing up of the working foot to under the knee)

REVERENCE: A deep curtsy; performed at the end of class as a mark of thanks and respect

ROND DE JAMBE À TERRE: Circle of the leg on the ground; a barre exercise in which one leg moves in a semicircle on the ground

SAUTÉ: To jump off the ground with both feet

SISSONNE: A scissor-like movement where the dancer jumps from two feet to one foot, or from two feet to two feet

TEMPS LEVÉ: Raised movement; a sharp jump on one foot

TENDU: Stretched; held-out; tight (in which a leg is extended straight out to the front *devant,* back *derrière,* or side *à la seconde,* with the foot fully pointed)